I0712691

Innerworld

A Satire

ISBN: 979-8-9854960-2-4 (Hardcover)

Library of Congress Control Number: 2023932534

Any references to historical events, real people, or real places are used fictitiously. Names, characters, and places are products of the author's imagination.

Book design & format by Guardian Publisher.

Printed by Guardian Publisher, in the United States of America.

First printing edition 2022.

Guardian Publisher
30N Gould St.
Sheridan, WY, 82801

www.jceganauthor.com

DEDICATION

For Heather and Robyn and David, who love books

ACKNOWLEDGEMENTS

First of all, as always, there are too many people to thank, so if I miss someone who should be here, my heartfelt apologies and I hope I'm quite thorough. I thank my publishing team: Publishing consultant, Bracken Joseph, Illustrations by Mohsin Ali (Digital artist at The Guardian Group of Companies) Project Head Simran Hans (Book and Film Critic at The Guardian, The New York Times and New Statesman.) I thank my agent and editor Steve and Ruthie Hutson. I thank wholeheartedly Kevin M. Kraft for his encouragement, friendship and kinship in all things fantastic and in our shared Christian faith. I thank Lisa Younger, Melissa Shaffer and Kenneth King for being my first beta readers. I thank all the other beta readers, who loved this book, and laughed and gave such wonderful reviews. I thank Melinda King for encouraging me to write more, and I will, and am. I thank my family for pushing me to finish, even among the most distressing and difficult of times, for each of us has a sorrow, and a joy to share with one another. Some of my beta readers have moved on to a world I can only imagine is more fascinating, more beautiful and satisfying a place to exist than any other dimension, real or imagined, for they are now with the Creator of all things, and holds all things together. Special thanks to Caleb Kaltenbach, his encouragement even during times of grief. Oh, I can't forget to thank Rob, Bryan, Marty and Terry, who have been looking forward to this book and who have greatly shaped my world view. May this book lighten your hearts, bring a smile, a laugh, and the same sense of awe reading it as I had writing it during dark days and light days.

CONTENTS

	Foreword by Kevin M. Kraft	1
	Prologue	3
1	The Boy Who Didn't Die Yet	4
2	The Beautiful Woman All Dressed in White	14
3	It's Not Just News	24
4	Two Rays and a Forrest	32
5	Clement Stebbs	38
6	First Order of Business	44
7	They Come When it Rains	50
8	The Quest	58
9	The Purpose	64
10	A Parting Party	70
11	Fog and Spectacular News	78
12	Giant Schlurrgs	84
13	Sizable Quantum Vortexes	90
14	The Influence of Politikus Mediosus	96

15 The Battle of Marsdon Hill   102

16 Potty Harrison and the Chamber of Commerce   108

Epilogue   120

End Notes   123

Map of *Innerworld*   124

About The Author   126

FOREWORD BY KEVIN M. KRAFT

I wish I had met James "J.C." Egan when I was a child. I think he and I would have been best friends. It is indeed a rare joy to meet someone with whom one shares an affinity. I have been writing fiction for a long time- science fiction, fantasy, drama, comedy, or some combination thereof. However, having known Mr. Egan for only a year or so, I already perceive him to be a kind and thoughtful man with a sense of humor as warped as my own and as vivid an imagination, well familiar with the work of Burroughs, Verne, and Bradbury, with a healthy touch of Douglas Adams. Like me, he was influenced by television shows like *Twilight Zone, Night Gallery,* and *Kolchak the Night Stalker* and classic creature feature films like *Frankenstein, The Beast From 20,000 Fathoms* and the *Sinbad* series.

His imagination so thoroughly steeped in fantastic media, it was inevitable J.C. would seek to replicate the awe, adventure, and wit he had consumed in his writing, over time writing novels and plays and eventually working in the entertainment industry, most notably stage work as a writer, performer, producer, director and musician. He has worked in one way or another with such entertainment legends as Dick Van Dyke, during a Christmas tree lighting ceremony being his right hand man as he read *'Twas the Night Before Christmas.* Doug Jones on their worship team at church, Doug singing and J.C. on bass, and Walter Koenig in a few stage productions-just to name a few. I admire his abilities and the ease with which he appears to spin tales that often communicate his sense of humor and his Christian faith. With fictional intrepid reporter Carl Kolchak, from the 70's *Kolchak the Night Stalker* TV series as his social media profile picture, I suspected we might have things in common, especially a love for monsters! Yet, despite being so busy, J.C. took time to read my award-winning creature feature novella, *MOMO: An Inspirational Thriller,* giving it high praise. He also contributed his childhood memory of the Midwest cryptic phenomenon for my author's website. In fact, one could say that we have the Missouri Monster himself to thank for introducing two likeminded creatives and sprouting a friendship that I have come to enjoy and greatly appreciate for over a year now.

J.C. and I also share a love for music. He has written his share of stage musicals. Similar to C.S. Lewis, J.C. even includes the lyrics to original songs in some of his novels, when appropriate. So to say he is well-versed in different methods of storytelling would be an extreme understatement.

That being the case, as you crack open Innerworld, I hope that you will not only enjoy young Peter Harrison's magical inner worldly adventure but appreciate the rich, kaleidoscopic mind in which the rich characters and situations were divined.

No, I never knew James "J.C." Egan as a child. But I know him now, and I enjoy his work.

And I'm betting you will as well.

-Kevin M. Kraft, award-winning author of MOMO: An Inspirational Thriller

PROLOGUE

Bright Lights is an unassuming little town in the Mid-West of the United States. It has a river that runs through it and a large enough downtown to be called a downtown. There are movie theaters, churches, schools, shops, and business centers, like every small town. There's even a riverboat where people can play cards for money. A silly thing to do, because most people lose the games and thus lose the money, but they do it anyway.

Not a very remarkable town, to be sure, except it has the one distinction that no other town I know of has: a terrible history with the fantastic.

This is just one story about a person who had something wonderful and frightening and exhilarating happen to him.

- J.C. Egan

THE BOY WHO DIDN'T DIE YET

In a hole in the ground there was a boy. It wasn't a very nice hole in the ground. It wasn't your conventional multi-roomed, smooth-tunneled, have a fire in the fireplace and tea in the kettle boiling and cakes in the oven baking type of hole. No, this was a dank, smelly, muddy, wormy and totally unacceptable hole and the boy was stuck in it. His name was Peter Harrison but all the children at his school called him Potty because he often had to use it. Since most school children about his age, in and around twelve years, are terribly cruel, the nickname stuck, and Peter was always, even after his medical treatments, known as Potty.

How Potty got into this hole is probably easy to figure out. The very same cruel classmates thought how much fun it would be to throw someone down a well during their dull and rather short lunch time. Who better to toss around than Mr. Potty Harrison?

"No one better!" they thought. So Clement Stebbs, the one who felt more than any of the other children that he had a right to throw anyone down anything, gathered a collection of the most insecure and bully-ish of the classmates and decided to have a go at it.

Therefore, Peter was unceremoniously picked up, carried up in the air over the asphalt that was supposed to be the playground of Ewart Street Elementary School, out the swinging and squeaking chain link gate, (that someone always managed to break open, leaving the poor groundskeeper to constantly replace the lock, which on this day, hadn't been done yet) and up the dry, burnt-grass hill to the well that no longer had a bucket. Into the well was cast the little twelve-year-old boy with the irritable bowel syndrome. He landed with a crack and a thud. A moist, muddy thud and a definite "I might have broken something in my leg" crack. Three hours had already passed, and by dinnertime he had not returned home, not to mention his teachers were all wondering what had happened to him.

Peter lived with his grandmother and she was a kindly woman, a little absent-minded, and plump around the middle, but kindly nonetheless. She really never understood why Peter would come home from school angry all the time. Sometimes he would come home crying. Perhaps he has a cold, was what she thought or perhaps he still has tummy trouble. Whatever the reason Peter never really told her it was because the children at school made him suffer terribly, especially Clement, who was probably just as upset because of his awful name. By this time of day, however, no matter what his mood, he would always be home. She was starting to worry. Her name was Mrs. Nora Nesbitt, but everyone on the block where she lived called her Grandma. Peter was her daughter's child and Peter was living with Mrs. Nesbitt because his mom and dad had had a very unfortunate accident.

The parents of Peter Harrison, Wilhlemina Nesbitt Harrison and Argyle Perciville Harrison, were really wonderful as far as parents were concerned but like Mrs. Nesbitt, they were terribly absent-minded when it came to the important things in life. Argyle worked for a private firm that made some kind of technical device that did something or other and Wilhelmina worked for the city, filling out forms and helping people with their taxes. These seemed like important jobs and as such they were.

But Peter had thought, why are they so absent-minded about things around the house?

Peter's mom and dad had left one of the devices Argyle was building in the garage plugged into a bad outlet and one Sunday, while Argyle and Wilhelmina were about to be on their way to a picnic luncheon with some of her clients, the darn thing went up in a cloud of green and pink smoke, taking the small Ford convertible car and Argyle and Wilhelmina with it. The explosion could be seen all over the neighborhood as clear as day and as far as Naperville, and that was far. This had all happened when Peter was nine, and now he was twelve.

The last thing Mrs. Nesbitt needed now was to have her grandson go missing. The explosion three years earlier had been shown all over television. The car, Argyle, and Wilhelmina had never been found. This had been a terrible tragedy for Peter and Mrs. Nesbitt, but she felt that Peter somehow took the blame upon himself. Children who lose parents at that age often do. So, she tried to make her home a happy place for Peter, despite his medical troubles and whatever was making him sad or angry. She felt whatever she was doing wasn't working and started to panic.

"Where is he?" she kept asking herself. "He has never been this late. He is always home in time for supper."

Mrs. Nesbitt had no idea at that very hour Peter was lying in an abandoned well just outside Ewart Street Elementary. "Oh dear," she continued, "I suppose I better call the police." She untied the apron she wore around her ample middle and wiped her hands on it, placing it on the counter near the dish-filled sink, and grabbed the phone. She dialed for emergency help and waited patiently.

Meanwhile, in that dank, dark and smelly hole, Peter realized the pain in his leg was not really a break. He had landed on some roots that were coming up through the ground, and one had snapped. Still, he ached all over and his leg was numb. Peter stood up and took a look around, standing gingerly on his two feet, favoring the sore leg. It tingled as if it had been asleep. After a few seconds the feeling started to return and he could stand with better balance than before and looked directly above him. The afternoon light was peeking through a tiny hole the size of a baseball.

That must be the top of the well, he thought. I'll never get out of here. There is no way to climb out. Indeed, there wasn't. There were no handrails, no jutting stones, no vine creepers or anything of the like. Peter just stood there and stared at the rounded wall in front of him. He looked all around the well and found that the wall was a smooth, slick and slimy curved surface. There was nothing to show any change in the structure of the well all around him except for one tiny thing. At the bottom of the well, directly behind him, there was a thin sliver of light. It was much like the light that would shine under a door when the light on the other side of the door was turned on and the light on your side of the door was shut off. The light wasn't particularly bright, but it was very intriguing.

Peter turned completely around so he wasn't straining his neck and faced that side of the well that had the strange light on the floor and knelt down to take a look.

"Yep," he said out loud, "there is a crack in the wall of this well. It must be some kind of door." He tried to stick his fingers through the crack but they were too big. He stood up and started knocking on the wall of the well and heard a hollow sound as if he was knocking on a wooden door, even though the wall at the first touch felt like stone. He tried knocking on another part of the well and the sound was much more like hitting a rock. Again, he tried knocking on the other part of the well that he felt might be a doorway. Not much happened and it was getting darker so he thought he'd run his hand along that section of the well wall and see if he could feel a latch or something. All he felt, after what seemed like an eternity searching, were little rocks or pebbles that were sticking into the well wall. He started to press on them and then suddenly, to his surprise, one moved into the wall like a button on a machine. There was a still silence and Peter held his breath. The light in the floor started to grow a little wider at one end. It was the effect of a door opening, which indeed was what was happening. That section of the wall slid inward, like a door on a hinge, but made a monstrous noise like two boulders rubbing together. Peter couldn't believe his eyes; right in front of him was a doorway. It opened to a small landing made of old flagstone and covered in green moss. From this landing there was a staircase that wound itself down-ward to some other chamber.

Peter took a deep breath and limped in because his leg still hurt. The doorway remained open, which gave him some comfort; he didn't want it closing behind him and keeping him from the only way out of the well. How-ever, if he could get back, he still had no way to get out to the top. He decided to walk down the stairway but it was getting very dark and he didn't have a flashlight. With what little light he had and with his hand on the wall to his left he gingerly stepped down the winding staircase that wound around to his right when suddenly and with a great thud the door behind him slammed shut.

The noise made Peter stop and try to catch his breath because the sound of it was so startling. Also, on top of being startled he was terribly afraid that he was trapped. There was hardly any light to see by except for a sort of ghostly glow that was coming from down the stairs.

Funny, he thought, *that light should be brighter somehow. It seemed to be when I was on the other side of this door.* Peter slowly turned around and went back and tried the door but it was shut fast. *Well, that's no good. I guess I must continue on.* He shivered and felt very much like he wanted to use the bathroom just then, but after taking a few deep breaths he moved forward ever so cautiously.

He descended one step at a time with his left hand feeling the wall next to him and helping to keep him steady. It seemed to take forever and ever and many times Peter got so tired that he would just sit down and try to rest. It took all his strength to keep from crying but he managed, and after a time he would stand up again and continue down the stairs. The ghostly light way down the passageway looked to Peter like it wasn't getting any brighter as he expected it should. It wasn't getting dimmer either and that was at least a comforting thought. He sat down again and tried to reason things out in his brain.

Surely the kids at school were not cruel enough to leave him in the well to die so they should have gone back to get a teacher or someone to come and help by now. Clement could be mean, but he wasn't about to let someone die. Unless he got scared. Oh, that would be just the thing. He'd get scared and think that he'd get into a heap of trouble, which he would, so he probably wouldn't say anything to anybody. Grandma certainly would be calling the school to find out where he was because it was at least passed dinnertime. Then he remembered the school was probably closed. After thinking like this for what seemed an hour or more, he stood up and continued down the winding staircase, careful to keep his hand on the wall.

Just when he thought he was going to have to sit down for another rest his feet hit what felt like a dirt floor.

Goodness, he thought. *I must have hit bottom.* It was now very dark and Peter was very scared, but the glow of light he had been following hadn't dimmed and he could almost tell that whatever was making the light was but a few feet in front of him. He started to walk toward it. By this time, he had really been perspiring and his feet hurt and he had to go to the bathroom so badly, but all those unpleasant feelings fell away when he saw clearly what was before him. It was an archway made of old gray stones. It was very tall and on either side of the archway, lodged in the pillar of stones that helped form the arch, were torches: long poles with some mossy-like substance on the tips that were on fire and giving off the glow he had seen. At the apex of the arch, the center of the top, there was a legend written out in some strange language that he didn't understand and using strange letters that he had never seen; but they looked wonderfully weird in the torchlight. He felt somehow this was either a written warning or instructions on what to do when one walked under the arch.

"I wonder if I should walk through it," he said aloud. He peered through the arch to see what was on the other side but all he could see was inky black gloom. He called, "Hello!" but no one answered. All he heard was an echo and he knew enough about echoes to know there was a chamber on the other side of that arch and maybe not much more.

"Well, there's no use standing here guessing," he said to himself. "So, I might as well just bite the bullet and walk through it." "Bite the bullet" was just an expression he had heard his grandma use when trying to pull hairs out of her chin. Peter didn't actually have a bullet to bite. He reached up and grabbed the torch on his left and slowly walked through the arch.

He didn't feel anything strange or think that he might have been dreaming and waking up, but in an instant, he was in a wooded glen. He immediately turned around to see the arch he passed through and it looked much farther away than it should have been. It was there, however, and through the archway he could just make out the bottom of the winding staircase he had come down. He looked back in the direction he was walking and noticed the wooded glen was bright, as if it were noon. He looked up toward the sun, but instead, through a mist of what could have been clouds, he could make out what looked like the ceiling of an immense cave. He dropped his torch, which had gone out without his knowing it.

"Why I'll be," he said. "I've managed to come into an underground world. How unlikely and slightly unnerving." He sat down in the soft, springy grass and covered his eyes. After a time, he opened them and he was still in the beautiful wooded glen. There were trees of all kinds, and bright yellow and red and purple flowers dotting the ground all around him. He was sitting on the most wonderfully soft and springy grass that was so green, and seemed to go on and on before him for miles. The trees towered above him, reaching up toward that far away ceiling of rock that wouldn't be noticeable through the clouds if you weren't really looking for it. It was almost as if there was a sky above him. There was sunlight but where it was coming from, he couldn't tell.

After a while some rabbits started rummaging around in the grass. They must have had warrens nearby and Peter stayed very still to see what they would do.

Astonishing! An underground world with animals! The rabbits didn't take any notice of him until he sneezed. They scattered at the sound and Peter felt lonely again.

The loneliness settled into a small tinge of regret. Although for the life of him he couldn't really focus on what he really regretted, because he hadn't done anything significantly wrong; not in his recent memory, anyway. So, the regret progressed to a state of depression and kind of swam around his insides looking for something to irritate.

Well, I'm all alone, he thought, *my friends hate me. For what I don't know,* was his second thought. *To be honest, I have no friends,* was what he finally concluded and the depression found something to swim with; to tear apart and shake up and swallow whole like a large voracious shark in a tiny backyard pool.

"This won't do," said Peter aloud. "I'm just dreaming. This is a hallucination. That's all it is. In the morning I'll wake up dead and it will all be over." He started to cry.

"Oh, dear! I don't want to wake up dead!"

Then he immediately stopped crying. Something was happening to his insides. He no longer had the urge to use the loo, but the depression that was eating away at him suddenly turned to ire. He was angry and he wasn't going to take it anymore.

Peter stood up to his full height of five feet and almost an inch extra. He wasn't a remarkable looking boy. He had an average build for his age and an average small amount of tub for his height. There was nothing about him to distinguish him from other boys his age. He scratched his sandy colored hair and looked around again.

The meadow he was in was astonishingly beautiful.

"How could this be? I must be crazy!" he said. "If I'm going to be insane, I might as well enjoy it and go exploring; that is at least what a dying kid should do, go on an adventure." So, Peter wiped the tears from his brown eyes and started off into the heart of the meadow, not knowing what would happen next.

At home Grandma Nesbitt was in more than just a tizzy; she was downright hysterical. She had several police officers at the door and two out in the neighborhood roaming the streets looking for an average brown-eyed, sandy-haired boy with no visible scars. The teachers and principal of Ewart Street Elementary were all upset and frantic. Someone was going to get fired. The school was going to be sued. Some children who could be implicated in the disappearance of Potty would probably end up in juvenile hall, again. This was a rotten day altogether.

"Did Potty…" started one of the officers in the doorway; he was speaking to Grandma Nesbitt.

"Peter," she corrected him.

"Sorry, I meant Peter. Did he have any favorite places he liked to hide? An old refrigerator for instance, that he could lock himself up in and slowly suffocate to a pale shade of blue?"

Mrs. Nesbitt started to cry.

"Again, I apologize, but really it would help us a lot if we knew of someplace, he liked to hang out and be alone."

"I know of someplace." The voice that said this did not belong to Mrs. Nesbitt or to any of the other adults in the house. It came from a small girl whose nickname was Bucky and who had wandered into the house. She went to Ewart and was also quite a loner. Why she had the name Bucky no one knew, no one ever asked, but I can tell you it had something to do with her teeth.

"What?" asked Mrs. Nesbitt.

"Yes, Grandma Nesbitt," said Bucky, trying hard not to show her prominent front teeth by keeping a very solemn look on her face. "I believe some of the boys at school may have…" she trailed off.

"Please," said the officer in charge, "tell us what you know." Bucky smiled quickly, and then stopped again when the officer looked away, suppressing a grin.

"Some of the boys don't like Peter. They weren't very pleasant to him today. Apparently, there is this old haunted well at the top of Marsdon Hill."

There was a collective gasp.

"Marsdon Hill?" asked one of the other police officers. "Not the old haunted well at the top of Marsdon Hill?"

"I thought," started another officer, "that the well up on Marsdon Hill was abandoned. That there hadn't been a ghost living in there for, oh I don't know, two or three years."

"Gentlemen, please!" pleaded Grandma Nesbitt. "Let the young girl finish. Go on dear, and try not to smile."

Bucky continued. "Apparently, Potty, I mean Peter, was not too keen on the well, what with it being haunted and all."

"Allegedly," added the officer in charge. "We have to be careful of these things you know."

"Yes," continued Bucky, being very solemn, "we have to be careful. The other boys didn't care and I think they picked up Peter and threw him down the well."

There was silence for just a moment. Then everyone burst out laughing.

"Ha!" said the officer in charge. "Who ever heard of throwing a kid in a well? That sounds positively Biblical and we all know how wrong that can be."

"Yet," added Bucky, "I saw it."

"Sure, you did," said the officer in charge and then he patted her on the head. "Sure, you did, young person. What an imagination. No, I think we need to search around for old abandoned refrigerators and forget completely the idea of a kid getting stuck in a well."

"Fairy tales," said another officer, who wanted a promotion.

"Yes, Smithers," replied the officer in charge, "fairy tales, indeed."

Smithers smiled broadly. Unlike Bucky, he had no front teeth, and he didn't care.

Bucky looked up at Mrs. Nesbitt. "You do believe me, don't you Grandma?"

"Oh, Deary, don't look at me like that, with your mouth open. Of course, I think I could believe you, but these are professional men here. I don't know but it does sound awfully fairy tale like to be thrown into a well by a group of bullies."

So, Peter was stuck at the bottom of a well, either having a dream or really living a true, bona fide fairy tale of his own. He wouldn't know until all of it was over. All he knew was the deeper into the meadow he walked, the more like the real outside it seemed, and he turned his head this way and that, not looking where he was going. So, the last thing he expected was to bump into a beautiful woman all dressed in white, but he did, and it hurt his head so he had to sit down.

"Welcome, Potty," said the beautiful woman all dressed in white.

"The name is Peter," said Peter, rubbing his head.

"Welcome, Peter. I am," she was about to make a proclamation.

Peter waited anxiously. Was she an angel? Was he really dead? If this was heaven, why was it underground? If it were a dream, would he wake up? If this were a real fairy land would there be any homework? So many thoughts ran through his head as she continued to speak.

"I am," she said, "the Beautiful Woman All Dressed in White.".

THE BEAUTIFUL WOMAN ALL DRESSED IN WHITE

Peter was impressed, but suddenly very tired, and he couldn't stay awake any longer. He fell into a deep slumber right there in front of the Beautiful Woman All Dressed in White and dreamed of grabbing at a very thin thread with a very giant fist. He didn't know why.

Peter awoke from his dream stifling a scream. His mouth was dry and his head was dizzy, as if he'd come out of a bad flu. He looked around and noticed it was so dark he couldn't see beyond anything. It was as if someone had put a black cloth over his eyes. He squinted, he opened his eyes wide, he shook his head; yes, there was something over his eyes. He reached up and pulled a piece of what was probably black cloth off his face. It didn't help much; he was still in the dark.

There was something, though, something about where he was that he didn't like. It was like a memory of long ago and it gave him a very bad feeling. He couldn't quite put his finger on what it was. Was it his bed? No, he was lying on soft, sweet-smelling grass. Was it his room? No, because as his eyes grew accustomed to the dark, he noticed his walls looked like canvas or muslin. It could very well be a tent. He could see a gray light coming through the flap of the tent in front of him. Perhaps it was dawn. There were sounds; they could be what was so unsettling. The sounds were crickets, and frogs and animals that reminded him of camping.

"That's it!" he yelled. "I hate camping."

Just then the flap to the tent, for that is what he was in, opened and in peeked a beautiful blond head of hair, bright green eyes and a rose red smile.

"Good morning, Potty."

"Peter."

"Peter."

"Who are you again, and where am I?"

The beautiful face just smiled at him. The smile parted slightly, revealing perfectly white and well aligned teeth. She was simply smashing.

"As I said yesterday, I am the Beautiful Woman All Dressed in White." She stepped slightly into the tent, showing off her white gown as if she were buying it at Marks and Spencer.

"Aren't I lovely?" There was no hint of egotism in her question, just the simple truth.

"I guess so. For a girl." That was all Peter could think of saying, but truthfully, she was indeed, very beautiful.

"Don't let my appearance fool you, Peter. Not all beautiful things are good. Not all things that are pleasing to the eye are to be trusted."

Are you to be trusted? he thought to himself.

As if she could read his mind, she answered his question. "You may wonder if I am to be trusted. You won't know until you've gotten to know me and this world better."

"I'm not sure," he started, "what I am doing here, or where I am, or if this is some sort of hallucination brought on by a severe head injury."

"It isn't."

"But how..."

"Trust me."

"But you just said..." Then she left him. The light was coming through the flap in the tent and it was obviously morning, and suddenly he smelled something wonderful. Again, he had a vague memory of when he was a little child, sleeping in his bed. The furnace was on so he had that comforting sound, and the smell of coffee brewing and bacon frying was so reassuring, that he thought for a moment he was again five years old, and safe at home with his mother. He stood up and noticed he was still dressed in his school clothes; they were a tad tight. He stepped outside through the tent flap ready to meet his hallucination. He again saw the beautiful green and brightly flowered landscape around him. There to his right was the Beautiful Woman cooking breakfast and just starting the pancakes.

"I believe this is a traditional morning meal in your world, if I remember right?" Behind her was a table, all laid out with delicious-looking fruit. There were ripe raspberries, blueberries, strawberries and an earthen jar of honey. There were small cakes and a large plate full of crispy bacon. There was white butter and cream, hot frothy chocolate in a beautiful pot and tall iced glasses of orange juice. The pancakes were at the cooking point where they smelled like he walked right into a fresh bakery that used real vanilla in its cookies.

"Now see here, whoever you are; I'm not falling for this nonsense." He really wanted to sit down and eat, but he was going to be assertive if he could. At the table were two chairs. Obviously, she was to join him for breakfast.

"What nonsense? I'm trying to make you feel at home."

"It hurts."

"What? What have I done to hurt you?" She really looked concerned. He couldn't see a trace of deception in her face, and her own eyes started to water.

"It reminds me of my mother."

"Isn't that good?"

"She's dead. You know."

The Beautiful Woman turned away from Peter, and started to wipe her eyes dry. "I can take it all away from here, if you wish. The table, the food I mean. All of it." She turned back to him, and had obviously been crying harder. "Good memories, however, though they might bring grief, are still good. Not all ugly things are bad, Peter. Some help. I am not a hallucination. I am not a dream of your mother. But I am a friend, and now that these pancakes are cooking, and smelling so wonderful, I would be honored if you would have breakfast with me."

Peter looked down and shuffled his feet. He felt a little embarrassed. He quietly walked over to the table and pulled out a chair for himself.

"May I sit down?"

"You are indeed, a polite young man. Of course, you can."

He sat down. Then thought again and immediately stood up, walked around to the other side and pulled out the chair for her. She laughed; a lilting, musical laugh, and set the plate of pancakes on the table. She then sat down with a, "Thank you, you are very kind," and then waited for Peter to take his seat. Peter sat down and then the Beautiful Woman closed her eyes for a good few seconds and, wearing a simply pure and happy smile She opened her eyes and looked at Peter.

"I'm grateful," she told him.

He nodded but wasn't really sure what she meant and then looked around him. There was something wrong.

"What is it?" she asked.

"There's no maple syrup."

She had to close her eyes and wrinkle up her nose for a moment, as if she were trying to remember something for a test, and then opened her eyes up again, with a look of surprise on her face.

"Oh, I know what that is! Look into the jar next to the honey."

There was no jar next to the honey when Peter first looked on the table, at least as far as he could remember; but now it was there. He opened it and the most mouth-watering pure maple syrup was inside. After he had a plateful of pancakes smothered in this wonderful syrup, and a bowl full of cream and blueberries and a couple of slices of bacon, he started to cry.

"Change, especially drastic change, is not easy to take. You've had a shock. It is all right to cry." She handed him a handkerchief.

"But," he began, "I'm not really here. This is a dream. This kind of thing doesn't happen to people. To me. I was thrown down a well. I must have hit my head."

"So, you do come from Outerworld, as I had guessed." She was very pleased with herself, as if she got the right answer in school.

"I'm from Bright Lights. Near Naperville. Near Chicago."

She kept looking at him with that look of childlike glee at spelling a word correctly.

"Illinois," he continued.

"That all sounds like Outerworld to me." She started to clean up.

"Where are you going to put all the dirty dishes?"

"In the tent. Isn't that where they go?"

"They have to be cleaned first."

"They are."

And so, they were. Peter was amazed.

"Well, if this is a hallucination, then I'm all for it. It's just too cool."

"I can make it warmer," she said.

"No," he started to correct her, "cool means great, or excellent, in, in Outerworld language." He then thought about how confusing the English language can be. "But it also means the absence of heat, or such," he said, hastily.

"How amusing!" She laughed again. "So, you believe me, then?"

"No, but I'm willing to play along until someone comes to the well and takes me to a hospital."

"You are strange, but I believe in you." She laughed that infuriating little musical laugh again.

Peter was silent for some time. He looked up at her. She had moved away from the table and was putting the very clean dishes into the tent.

After what seemed like an eternity, he spoke up.

"Are you an angel?" he asked.

She turned and looked at him. She smiled.

"What's an angel?"

Peter thought for a moment.

"We put it on the top of our Christmas tree."

"Now, I don't go on top of trees."

He thought again for a moment. That was a silly thing to say.

"I don't know how to put it. You know, I'm only twelve. I would say an angel is an invisible being in fairy stories that helps people."

"No," she said. "I'm not invisible."

"I don't know how to say it."

"I am the Beautiful Woman All Dressed in White. That's how I know to say it. What more do you need?"

"Did you have a father and a mother?"

There was silence. She just looked at him. She seemed thoughtful, yet, very happy.

"I did, yes."

"Did they love you?"

"They did, yes."

"Did they die?"

"Yes."

"I'm sorry." Then Peter started to cry again.

"Death isn't the end, Peter, but cry if you must because grief will cease. But you have a great day ahead of you. A great day and a great task."

She finished putting the plates into the tent, and then pulled out the center pole. The tent pulled into itself and into the top of the pole it went, like a collapsible umbrella. She then was able to collapse the pole in the same way, and put it into her lovely white handbag she wore around her shoulder, which, according to Peter's memory, wasn't there before.

"Why," he started to ask forcefully, trying to sound like a grown man, "am I here?"

The Beautiful Woman motioned for him to sit down as she prepared to fold up the table. He did so, and waited until she stuffed the folded (like an old-style travel map) table into her lovely handbag.

"I hope, Peter, that you are here to help me."

Peter was astounded.

"Help you? How can I help you? I'm not magical or anything. I'm just a chubby kid!"

The Beautiful Woman looked like she was thinking rather hard. She sat down in the chair opposite him, because she hadn't put it away yet.

"I'm not sure what you know and what you don't know. Perhaps we'll discover it together today, but I have to take you to the Sea of Folsborn. That is where you will meet the ship that will take you ultimately to the Temple of Situational Ethics. That lies in the dark land of Covenswold. A very evil place. No one should dare to go there alone."

"Why go there at all?"

"Follow me, Potty."

"Peter."

"Peter. We'll talk on the way."

Peter didn't stand up. He sat there for a moment and thought about what she just said.

"I really would rather go home."

"Perhaps this is the way?" she posited.

"Well," he started, "if this is some lucid dream…"

She looked at him strangely.

"A term I learned in fifth grade beginning psychology. They teach us weird stuff at school."

"Ah," she said.

"As I was saying, if this is some lucid dream, then it should be fun. It's my imagination, and I find it engrossing."

She looked at him again with the same quizzical expression.

"English and grammar, advanced."

"Are you considered bright in Outerworld?"

"No. We have to learn it whether we understand it or not. It's the rules."

"I think you are very bright." She stood up and took his hand, and when he stood, the chairs were no longer there. She started to walk away from what was their camp, to a small hill in what looked like a westerly direction, for the morning light came from the opposite way.

Without telling him much, except certain trivial information about the birds, the types of trees, all the kinds of flowers and such, they continued to walk westward. They stopped once or twice for a break, but Peter was feeling very fit by this time, and didn't need any frequent stops like he often did when on a field trip with Ewart Street Elementary.

The sun climbed into the hazy sky, (for indeed, there was a sun, or something like it) obscuring any visible signs that they were in some immense cavern, and it also became very hot. They decided to stop for lunch.

"It is time to stop for launch," said the Beautiful Woman.

"I think you mean lunch."

Again, she screwed up her face as if she were trying to do algebra without a pencil and paper and then exclaimed, "Ah yes! Lunch!"

She reached into her handbag and pulled out two roast turkey sandwiches, some crunchy nuts and a jug of lemon flavored something or other. It tasted like real lemon juice but sweet with a touch of grape. It was, simply put, amazing.

"You must have strength, Peter, if you are to find the three magic vessels."

"Oh good, I get to know what I'm supposed to do." He ate his sandwich, which tasted very smoky, like bar-b-cue, and took a large swig of the lemony grape drink. "I must find the three magic vessels. And they are?"

"Magical," she answered. "And they are three. That's right."

"But what do they look like?"

She laughed again, but it wasn't quite as infuriating, since Peter decided, he was going to enjoy his own madness.

"I have no idea. That's why you're here. You know these sorts of things."

Peter was shocked. He looked around him; everything was still just as clear and real as if he were awake. Certainly, if this were a dream, he would have done better with whatever quest he needed to go on.

"Can't I just throw a magic ring into the fire, or, say, slay a dragon, or something more along the lines of what I've read? Can we go see the wizard instead?"

The sky suddenly darkened and the Beautiful Woman's face turned sour. She didn't look evil; just very stern and important, like a doctor.

"No! We must not see him together. You must not ask that of me again. You will know what to do as you do it. When we get to the Sea of Folsborn, you will start your quest, and begin the tasks, but don't ever 'wish' to see such a person."

"So, there is a wizard? Why can't we see him?"

She said nothing. She finished her lunch, drank a bit of the juice, and let Peter finish it off. They stood up and began walking again.

For a long time, they walked in silence. Then they crested a grassy knoll, only to find sand and stiff weeds on the other side. They were nearing a beach. Peter could smell the salt air, and hear the breakers in the distance.

"We must be at the Sea of Folsborn."

"We are here."

She led the way down to the shore. The beach was part of a large cove, and off to Peter's right and jutting way out into a magnificent sea, was a promontory of rock. Anchored off the rock was, for all practical purposes, a very large rock or lot of land. This was covered with all sorts of flowers and plants, logs and rocks and crowded with tall timbers, or even trees, several of which reached up into the sky as if they were masts. However, the most amazing thing was the sea itself. It was gold, white and gray, but not a dull gray, and the waves billowed, rolled and crashed on the promontory and sluiced up the sand toward Peter's shoes. It looked like ginger ale, or something similar. Peter reached down toward the sand, got a handful of water and brought it to his lips. It was sea water all right. A real, honest to goodness underground ocean, laid out before him. It was astounding; the scope of it could not be comprehended.

"I'm afraid."

The Beautiful Woman let go of his hand.

"Don't be afraid of the water."

"It's not that. I'm afraid it is not real."

She looked confused again.

"It must be difficult for people in Outerworld to believe in things they don't see until they are right upon them."

Peter didn't say anything. He looked toward the strange rock off of the promontory.

"That's the good ship Forrest. The ship will take you across the sea; from there you will know how to get to Covenswold. I will miss you."

Peter looked up at her and smiled.

"Of course. Of course, you can't go with me. That's always the case, isn't it? The grown-ups always leave the kids.

"Who said I was a grown-up? I like you, in my own fashion, am a child."

"You are not human?"

"I can't answer for sure."

"So, you are an angel?"

She squinted again.

"Depends on the definition you choose. I don't go on top of trees."

He laughed. "So, I'm supposed to go to that island out there?" He pointed toward the large tree covered mass listing on the waves out from the promontory.

"That is not an island, Peter. That is a ship."

"Well, then, off we go."

She took his hand again, and looked at him with solemn eyes. She made sure he was ready before she spoke, then, with the deepest sincerity, and no theatrics, she gave him her last bit of advice.

"Don't believe everything you see, Peter. Don't believe everything you read. Above all, don't believe everything you hear. Lies of omission are still lies. Logic is twisted, bent and formed to the whim of the logician. No one in Innerworld, or even in Outerworld, is as adept at transforming reason than Politicus Mediosus. Beware of him, Peter. He is cunning, he is strong, but he is wrong. You must have the truth to beat him, and beat him you must, for it is your world that is in peril, Peter. Your world. You must thwart his plan, even if it means destroying him. Can you do this? There is no one else. It has been foretold long, long ago that one from Outerworld would descend to Innerworld and defeat Politicus and his mechanizing. Are you he? If so, then you know what you must do. Find the three magic vessels, and empty them each, at the appropriate time. This you must. All depends upon it. If Outerworld falls, we have no sky."

"Ah. What about, you know, large pillars and stuff?"

"Do what you must."

"How will I find these three vessels?"

"Are you from Outerworld?"

"I don't know; I came down a well."

"Yes, you came down the well. The secret well to Innerworld and now you are here."

"I'm just a boy!"

"Come, come! There will be none of that nonsense here. You are not just a boy. You are also just a male. That's problem enough."

"See here..." He was indignant.

"Good. Good. You will need to stand up for yourself. There are many perilous paths before you. Stay on the most difficult..."

"What? Why?" He was starting to really get concerned.

"If this were to be easy, I'd do it."

"Well, why don't you?"

"It has been foretold, long, long ago..."

He stopped her, "Why someone from Outerworld?"

"You have something no one in Innerworld has, or ever will have."

"And that is?"

"Asthma."

Now he was really confused. "Asthma? I have asthma?"

"You don't have asthma?"

"No! I have a digestive problem..."

She had a faraway look in her eyes. They grew wide, as if, in her mind, she was searching. In all the fairy lands of all the universes and secret portals, someone, somewhere may have made a terrible mistake. She wasn't going to tell him.

"Good enough. On your way."

She shoved Peter closer to the waves.

"Have fun, Potty, I'm sorry, I mean Peter. Stay dry. Call me when it's over."

"How do I call you?"

"Isn't that the customary farewell in Outerworld?" She laughed a musical lilting type of laugh and vanished, as if she were nothing but floating dandelion seeds.

IT'S NOT JUST NEWS

The soft, blue, almost eldritch glow of the television reflected off the dark surface of the living room window. Bucky sat there, quiet, listening to the talking heads on television blab on and on about who was dating whom, how much it was going to cost to do something, who might upset some kind of election and who just got declared "not guilty" in a very nasty criminal trial. What Bucky cared about was Peter, and the fact that for the last day and night, no one knew where he was. He couldn't be found, and no one would listen to her.

She had spent the previous day at school hanging around the creaky gate that lead to the dry grassy hill where the haunted well was rooted. The only person who had noticed her was Clement, the short, curly haired preadolescent who hated his own name, and consequently gave nasty nicknames to others. She had known he was the instigator of yesterday's affair, but no one had listened to her.

"What are you hanging around here for, Bucky?"

"I hate that name, Clement."

He kicked some dirt.

"Looking for your boyfriend?"

"He's not my boyfriend."

Clement smiled. "So, you are looking for someone?"

"You know darn well," she had started yelling, "who I'm looking for. You and your cohorts threw him in the well."

Clement laughed and kicked some more dirt. "I don't know what you're talking about."

"I saw you!"

Clement stopped laughing. He had that, "give me your lunch

money" look he was so famous for, and stalked over to her.

"What exactly did you see me do?"

"I saw you walking down from the haunted well. You and your friends."

He stopped. His face had gone blank like when the TV goes out, and he just thought for a minute. He began to smile.

"That's all you saw?"

"That's all I needed to see."

"Well, heck! We play around that thing all the time. Morris dropped his basketball down there and we were trying to fish it out. Ha! You're full of fantasies, that's what you are. Haunted well! There were no ghosts when I went up there yesterday."

Suddenly she spoke, rather fast. "To do what?" She had thought she'd catch him at his own game.

"To get Morris' ball, you moron." He had walked away, laughing. About halfway to the gym building he had turned and looked at her, almost said something and kept on walking. Bucky had waited; then when it looked like Clement was gone, she ran as fast as she could up the hill and right to the well. She looked down in it, but couldn't see anything, not even the reflection of water that you sometimes can see when you look down a deep well. She called out to Peter, yelling down the well. There was an echo. She waited, and there was nothing more. She did it again, and heard the echo and waited. Nothing.

She must have spent nearly an hour calling to Peter, but there were no answers. She had gone home, and gone up the stairs to her bedroom and quietly cried herself to sleep.

That was yesterday. Today, nothing remarkable happened, and more toward evening Bucky was sitting in her small, stuffy living room with her mother, who was lying nearly asleep in a lounge chair next to the sofa where Bucky sat, soaking in the blue light of the big screen. Bucky's mother loved the news. She would sit mesmerized for hours, watching news program after news program. This particular evening there was absolutely nothing on the evening news about the missing boy.

"So that's about what we can expect for tomorrow, Angela."

"Thanks, Ted. Now to Phil, with weather."

"No, Angela, I just did the weather."

"Ah, yes, Ted, and you did a smashing job."

"Thank you, my little rabbit."

"What?"

"My little bunny?" Ted looked nervous.

"What did you call me?"

"Am I going to lose my job over this?" There was silence on the TV.

"Am I done?" said Ted. "I think I'm done." I'll just go home." Angela looked blank. These were two typical TV news anchors with bright smiles and well-shaped hair, dressed in smart, European suits and blouses with matching sweaters, and not conveying any sort of confidence whatsoever to the viewing public.

"Right. Now here's Phil with weather," said a confused and flustered Angela.

Phil, who had dark, shiny hair, now appeared on screen. "We just did the weather, Angela, but I can bring you traffic."

"I really don't care, Ted."

"Phil."

"I mean, Phil. Just say something."

Bucky reached over to her mother's chair to get the remote. Her mother was staring at the screen with the same glazed eyes that stared out at you from a lobster tank at a fancy restaurant. Bucky let her fingers touch the remote; there wasn't a stir from her mother. She let her thumb, gingerly, touch the side of the remote and still nothing happened. She gently put her whole hand on the remote and her mother said nothing. She quietly slid the remote off the arm chair, as if it were a bomb, and brought it closely to her face so she could read the dials.

"Ugh," her mother groaned.

"Yes?"

"Leave the news on. I want to hear about the TV star who lost his job because he acts like such a jerk. That's such good TV. Then there's a special about that heiress who got arrested and is now in rehab and I think she might finally get that tattoo she always wanted. I really want to see that."

Bucky just put the remote back on the arm of the lounge chair, got up and went into the dining room, small and dark, and looked out the glass sliding window to the tiny box of a back yard. The table fan, on the dining room table, was oscillating and making a quiet yet distinct vibrating noise.

The reflection of the power light from the fan looked like two little red eyes staring at her through the window.

"Mother, can we move the fan?"

"After the hot months are done."

"This is October."

"Why do you want to move the fan?"

"It creeps me out." Bucky turned to walk back in. She fell on the sofa and heaved a sigh.

"A fan creeps you out?"

"There are two beady, red, shiny eyes staring at me in the back yard window."

"That's the reflection of the power light on the fan."

"I know," said Bucky, without a little impatience. "It creeps me out.

Like some little creature is staring at me."

"Ha!"

"What? Don't tell me I'm paranoid. You've been saying that all day."

"You're not paranoid, dear. You're just realistic."

Bucky stood up in a huff and went upstairs to her bedroom. She lived alone with her mother, Gillian Newcastle, in a split-level town home near the west end of Bright Lights. She was only a block in one direction from Ewart's, and only a block in the other direction from Peter's house. Her room was as small as a cracker box almost. It was big enough for one little bed, a tiny dresser, two stuffed animals and a handful of story books. There was a window where the moon shone in too bright, and there was a photo of one of her favorite movie stars on her wall. The evening moon made it look gray in her room. It had been gray during the day, and it would be a dark and moody blue-gray during the night, for the clouds had rolled in, and rain was imminent.

She lay down on her bed until she heard her mom turn off the TV, climb the stairs and walk down the tiny hall to her own bedroom, and close the door.

Bucky got up, walked quietly downstairs, and went into the dining room. The fan was still on and the red light from its base still made the double reflection in the double paned window glass look like evil eyes, staring at her, watching her, to see if she would do something. She turned off the fan and the eyes winked out. Done.

Bucky then quietly went to the coat closet near the front door; she was still dressed in her school clothes. She took out her long black coat and checked to make sure the keys to the house were still in the pocket. Check. She then quietly opened the front door, turned the lock to keep anything out, and closed it behind her. Then she walked the long, dark, neighborhood block to Ewart's, and to the well.

It was cold, and a little misty. There was a slight fog on the ground, and if any little red eyes had looked out at her from the dark front windows of the houses she was passing, she'd faint away. But there wasn't anyone watching as far as she could see, and nothing made a sound. It was as quiet as a grave.

She almost slapped herself to keep from getting spooked.

Don't think about graves and red eyes and haunted wells until you get there, she thought to herself. Then Bucky did the bravest thing a girl her age could have done. She climbed the chain-link fence into the school yard near the gym, which was on the side of the street closest to her own, and she ran toward the squeaky gate that led to the well. It was swinging gently, as if someone had just run through it.

"Clement, no doubt," she said aloud. She now talked aloud to herself just to keep from running home. "He's probably waiting to throw me in the well." She stopped and looked around. It was absolutely still except for the swinging gate, but it wasn't swinging wide. It was a slow, kind of lazy swinging, like it was being moved by the wind, and there was a wind. The clouds had come in low, and there was mist, and there was fog, and now there was a breeze, a very steady breeze.

"It's just the wind, your silly girl," she told herself. "Time to go to the well."

She nearly fell over her feet as she ran up the steep and dusty hill to the well. It started to rain and the dirt and burnt grass and weeds would become muddy. She made it to the well, a typical stone thing with a wooden roof over it, but no bucket, and yelled down into it.

"Peter! Peter, are you there?" She listened. There was the echo, and then nothing.

"Peter! I need to know if you're all right!" Again, an echo and then empty air. She was really frustrated. The wind was blowing, the air was getting colder and the rain was starting to pelt. She turned to leave and just then, she thought she heard something down the well.

She turned swiftly and called again.

"Peter! Peter! Is that you?" She waited for the echo to subside. It was quiet. As she turned to go, for she was getting soaked, she distinctly heard, "No, it is not," coming from the well.

"There is someone down there!" She turned and looked in. She couldn't see anything in the dark.

"Who are you?" She waited.

"I'm not Peter."

"Are you all, right? Do you know where he is?"

"Yes."

"Yes, to both questions? Or to just one?"

There was silence.

"Yes."

Bucky was confused.

"Stay there and I'll get someone." She turned to leave.

"Peter."

Bucky stopped. She turned back. The voice sounded distant, like the wind. Maybe she was imagining it.

She thought she'd give it another try. "I need to know if Peter is down there." There was silence. Then, a small, far away voice like a breeze distinctly said, "Go home."

"What?" Bucky had a chill run down her spine.

"Go home," the breeze told her, "and lock the door."

That was it. Brave or not, she was getting nowhere here and that was just too spooky. She took off at a leap and slid down the muddy hill, getting sludge and weeds all knotted up in her socks, ran through the gate, but slipped on the asphalt playground and skinned her knees. With her eyes tearing up and the wind starting to really blow, she was afraid it might be a bad storm, even a tornado coming in. She stood up, took a deep breath and ran for home. Out of the corner of her eye she thought she saw Clement running as well, but there was no time to stop and ask questions.

After her long run, she stopped at her door and fiddled for her keys. Maybe they fell out when she climbed the fence to get home, she was in such a hurry, but no, there they were, and just in time, because the lightning in the sky was starting to flash, and in a second, the loud crack nearly deafened her. She opened the door, ran in and slammed it behind her, panting and trying to hold back tears. Her mother wasn't coming downstairs so she must really be sound asleep; that was a loud crack of thunder and a loud slam of the door.

Bucky took off her wet coat and hung it on the hall-tree by the door to dry, then she went to the stairs, but the fan in the dining room was on. Also, the TV had been turned back on and the voices coming from it were soft, as if the volume was turned low, but she could make out that it was again, just the news.

"I thought," again she was talking out loud, "that I had turned that fan off." She went into the dining room and sure enough, the reflection of the red lights looked like little imp eyes staring in at her. She turned the fan off. The light on the fan faded out. She turned to look out the back door window at the oncoming storm and froze in place. She took in a gasp of air and the hair on the back of her neck started to rise. There, through the double paned glass of the sliding back door window, were two little red, beady eyes, staring right at her.

Before she passed out, she heard Phil on the TV signing off, "Re-member Bright Lights, it's not just the news, it's SPECTACULAR!"

TWO RAYS AND A FORREST

Peter looked toward the hill where the Beautiful Woman All Dressed in White had been standing, and who just vanished like a bag of chocolate and white filling cookies that had been left on his kitchen counter. He sighed. He missed those cookies. He started to get a little perturbed and yelled out after her, though she had gone.

"Politicus Mediosus? That's what my subconscious came up with? You're kidding me!" He said aloud and was hitting his stride. "Couldn't I have thought of something cleverer? I sound like Edmund Spencer or John Bunyan! And I'm too young to know who those guys are!" He muttered under his breath. "Why couldn't I have had a normal schooling and learned, I don't know, home economics?"

He turned and looked at the rocky promontory ahead of him. It jutted out into the golden gleam of ocean; at least it looked and smelled like an ocean to him. He had only visited one once when he was little, but it was unmistakable.

"Another reason why I believe this is all in my imagination." He nodded and smiled to himself. "I'm literally off my rocker, so I might as well play along," he said, realizing he was talking to himself.

He climbed the rock, went over to the edge and saw there was a rope that he could walk on, with rope hand rails suspended by rope supports, extending out from the promontory to the island boat a few yards away. It looked hazardous.

"I say," said a voice from the island boat, "were you yelling at us?"

Peter shaded his eyes with his hand and he could see two figures standing on the island boat, near the railing of branches, looking out at him.

"No," he yelled back.

"Good, good. Because we don't know how to answer you," one of them replied.

Peter just stared. His eyes were getting accustomed to the light. He could just make out two old men, one tall and thin and one short and portly, grinning out at him.

"Are you just going to stand there, or are you going to come aboard?"

"You were waiting for me?"

"Yep," said the tall one. He didn't have much hair and Peter could see his shiny head quite well by now.

"Who told you I was coming?"

The shorter one stood on his toes.

"I saw you down on the beach, and figured you were coming to us, and well, we could use the fare."

Peter was a little disappointed. "I have no money," he yelled back. His feet hurt. His shoes were too tight.

"Can you cook?"

"I can make toast," said Peter.

"Good enough," said the taller one. That will give our wives a rest. We can't even make toast."

"I can," yelled the shorter one, who wore what looked like spectacles on his face.

"Yes, but not very well," countered the taller one.

Peter looked about. There was no one else with him; he had to make this decision alone.

"What the heck. Permission to come aboard?"

"Permission granted!" They both said in unison.

So, Peter took a step out onto the rope; it was firm and springy. After a few jumpy strides the rope looked and sounded like it was starting to fray, just possibly two feet ahead of him.

"Hang on," yelled the shorter one. "It will only take a second."

Just then the rope broke and his hand rails broke at the same spot. He was clinging onto a breaking rope hanging over the ocean and of course, he fell back against the rock with a thud and a scrape and a terrible jolt to his head. He kept his eyes open, hung onto his strand of rope and just dangled there against the rock, with the ocean water churning a few long yards beneath him. The broken piece of rope attached to the island boat fell into the water.

"Hang on, remember," yelled the shorter one again.

In an instant, the rope sprang up vertically and so did the broken piece on the other side, along with the respective handrails. Quite remarkably, they reattached themselves, as if they were growing together like some strange creeper vine that he saw on a nature show on television, filmed to look like high speed. As a result, he found himself sitting on the rope, hands on the rope rails, again extended over the ocean, his feet dangling over either side of the rope. He was safe--a little scraped and bruised, but safe.

"Good trick," he yelled out, nervously.

"Don't just sit there; we don't have all day," yelled the taller old man.

Peter carefully got to his feet. He looked down at the swirling, churning gold crested waves and thought to himself, *It's only cold ginger ale. I'll be fine. It's a dream, remember. A coma induced dream. You're in a lot more danger in real life, probably lying in a hospital bed muttering unintelligible sentences to anyone in the room: Grandma, Bucky, the doctor, the coroner...* His thoughts trailed off. He started to walk across the rope bridge again, a little slower, and feeling that it was sturdy beneath him, he picked up his pace.

He wanted to get across as fast as he could and get safely aboard the strange island ship, so with a bound he leaped the last yard and landed with a thud on what felt like real dirt.

"Ouch. I expected a wooden deck."

"Welcome aboard the Forrest," said the shorter man. "My name is Ray, and this is my best friend, Ray." He pointed to the taller one. They were about the same age but the taller one wasn't wearing spectacles and the shorter one wasn't bald.

"Hello," said Ray the Taller. "Welcome aboard."

Peter stood up and noticed he had scraped his shins. His pant legs were shorter than usual.

"Hello," he said, holding out his hand to Ray the Shorter. Ray took it, and they shook hands vigorously. Ray had a big grin on his ample face. Peter turned to Ray the Taller and held out his hand. Again, there was a very energetic handshake and lots of smiles from Ray the Taller and Peter certainly felt welcome.

"I'm Peter Harrison. Most of my friends call me Peter. Actually, that's not true. Most of my friends call me Potty, which isn't very nice."

"Why would your friends do that to you?" asked the taller one.

"They're not really my friends."

"Oh," said the shorter one, "well now you have two new friends who will call you Peter. So! You make toast, do you?"

Peter grinned. He liked these two men, but the warning from the Beautiful Woman all Dressed in White still went off inside his head. It was a low, muted, far away warning, as if it were a police siren on some lonely street far from his brain so it didn't really apply to him kind of warning; but it was there, nevertheless. Still, these men were kind, and even though there was a warning, there was also something warm and generous about them. Peter eventually came to the conclusion that if people were on the outside who they really were on the inside, then these two people would be the perfect example of warmth and friendliness.

He brushed off the warning and looked around him. This was the strangest boat he had ever been on, and he'd only been on one, and it was a row boat at the river near Bright Lights, and he got his shoes wet. This boat was really an island. It was as if it intentionally grew and shaped itself into a boat. The most remarkable thing was that even though it looked like it was made of dirt and rock, it floated like a real boat, it pitched and yawed (whatever that meant; Peter heard that term in a pirate movie he saw one Saturday morning on TV) like a real boat, but the deck was all grass and pebbles, sticks and rock, some flowers of a yellow and white kind and trees. Real, honest to goodness trees growing right out of the center of the deck, tall and majestic, unlike any trees he had seen, with leaves that intertwined with each other to give the impression they were not quite capable of functioning as sails, although they really would like to.

"How does this boat move?"

Ray the Shorter looked a little disappointed at Peter. He was still of the mind that maybe some toast and jam would be in the offing. Ray the Taller spoke up.

"Rather well. We haven't had it capsize or anything like that."

Ray the Shorter got his mind off of the toast and back in the conversation.

"We haven't even run aground, of course, because we essentially are the ground."

Peter looked at them both. Yep, these two were all right.

"But," he continued, "what motivates it?"

"Probably likes to swim," said Ray the Taller. "We call him the Good Ship Forrest. Because that's what he is. A good ship made out of a floating forest."

Peter took this all in, but it still wasn't helping him understand the basic principles of locomotion for this particular kind of vessel. He said as much, but the two Rays just looked at him with very comical but confused expressions.

"You're not from around here, are you?" asked Ray the Shorter.

"No sir. I'm not. If I am right in my thinking, well, it's rather complicated. This place only exists in my mind, like a dreamscape and you two are hyper-extensions of my subconscious ego."

Ray the shorter looked even more confused. He really wanted the toast now, because when he got confused, he got hungry. Lots of toast would be a big help, with butter and jam and something cool to wash it down with.

"Toast?"

Ray the Taller chimed in, "Well I don't know about all that. All I know is, Ray here, he and I have been friends since childhood and we've never met you until now so if we're part of your dream, well then, you've been asleep and dreaming longer than you've been alive."

Now this indeed made a great argument that maybe Peter wasn't hallucinating or dreaming at all, but then again, he looked at the impossible boat he was standing on. He shrugged.

"Where is the galley? I'd like to see if I could make the toast now."

Ray the Shorter nearly jumped with glee. He had to push his spectacles back up his nose because they almost fell off.

CLEMENT STEBBS

Bucky Newcastle woke up in semi-darkness. She was in a bed; that was for sure. She had a blanket up around her, tucked in firm and snug. There was a pillow under her head, but she was somehow not quite comfortable. Her eyes started to adjust to her surroundings and she realized why she wasn't as comfortable in this particular bed. It was because, indeed, it wasn't hers, but belonged to Bright Lights Droplet Hospital. A terrible name, she thought, for a hospital, but she was certain that was the one she was in, and there was an empty one next to left.

As her eyes adjusted better, she could see there was a small television mounted on the wall opposite the bed she was in, which was definitely a hospital bed because she could now see the railings on the sides of the bed and the wire buzzer (that you can press when you're in the hospital and you need to get a nurse) lying near her pillow. The TV was on, but the volume was really low. It sounded like terrible static and then she realized the sound she heard was her mother. Her mother was sitting in the chair in the corner by the window on her right. She was talking as if she were a news anchor, but very quietly so as not to wake Bucky up.

"It's not just news," she whispered, "It's SPECTACULAR."

That was a tough word to whisper but her mother managed and Bucky just sighed and quietly sat up. Why was she nervous? She had a nightmare probably. She was in the hospital; why? Did she get in some kind of accident? What was the last thing she remembered? The fan on the table and the red light; that was it, there was some connection there to the feeling of anxiety she was now experiencing. Her heart raced. She broke out in a cold sweat and wanted to call the nurse as the memory of that horrible creature in her backyard came flooding back to her brain.

Two little red eyes and some horrid bundle of flesh and nerves, small and squat with ugly knobby hands and claws for feet, as if it was something that fell off of an old cathedral but lived and breathed; that was what she remembered.

She went to press the buzzer for the nurse when she had that prickly feeling on the back of her neck. Someone or something else was in the room with her and it wasn't just her mother. She looked around and near the door to her hospital room, which was slightly ajar so there was a sliver of yellow light peeping through, was a living shape. It was still in shadow, so she couldn't quite make it out, but it looked like it had a large head.

"They're quite real," said the large head-shaped living creature.

This caused Bucky to want to scream, but she held her hand to her mouth and just stared. The dark of the room was starting to gray and she could just make out the shape in the corner. It was the shape of a boy, about her age. He was wearing a hat.

"I've seen them, too, but I haven't told anyone. Are you all, right?"

Bucky gave a startled silent yelp and caught her mouth with her hand again.

"Clement?"

"The nurse let me in. She's a nice person. Beautiful, really, in all that white."

"Why are you here? What am I doing here?" Bucky was starting to get really scared.

"I ran home after I heard that voice. As soon as you ran into your street, I saw one of those things, just sitting on the corner, looking at me. I thought it was an opossum, but it was not the same kind of ugly and it didn't have a tail."

"Why am I here?" she asked again.

"You fainted. Dead away. When your mom brought you here, apparently you were talking nonsense. Your mom told me all of this a while ago. You were asleep when I came in. I kind of feel responsible, a bit. I'm sorry. I shouldn't have scared you, and I shouldn't have done what I did to Potty. Poor guy. I wonder how he's doing down there, all alone in the rain."

"Shh," said Bucky's mom in a whisper, "there's a story about a debutant who divorced her husband after three days. Now that's important. I want to hear it."

Bucky smiled at her mother and then turned to Clement and whispered, "You need to tell the police."

"No one will listen. It's as if they think I'm lying. Believe me, I've tried."

Bucky thought for a minute, and remembered how hard it was for her to talk to the police at Peter's house the other day. Or had it been a week? She couldn't remember, it seemed so long. It was hard to believe it was only two days ago.

She turned on the light near her bed.

"Tell me everything I need to know," Bucky said to Clement. Before he could speak, however, the door opened and in walked the nurse.

Clement was right, she was beautiful, tall and all dressed in white like an old-fashioned nurse Bucky had seen in photographs. Her eyes were what was interesting and mysterious, for sometimes they seemed blue or green or not quite hazel. Her hair, under her old-fashioned nursing cap, when the light hit it just right, was blonde or slightly reddish, or when she stood in the shadows, brown. She was indescribable and that made Bucky uneasy. In fact, all the events of the last two days were so remarkable and jolting to her nerves, she thought she was going to pass out.

"You look out of place," said Bucky with a sigh trying, not quite too successfully, to not be dizzy.

The nurse was startled, as if she had been seen digging through the fridge for that forbidden piece of pie.

"How do you mean? What place should I be in?" the nurse replied, looking guilty.

"I don't know," Becky was getting frustrated, "maybe in 1965 or some other time."

"Oh!" The nurse was clearly relieved. "I thought you meant another dimension or something."

"What?" Bucky noticed Clement just stared and didn't say anything, so Bucky offered her question again, "What?"

"You know, different worlds, dimensions. There must be, oh," she wrinkled up her face as if calculating a terrible algebra problem, "dozens of other universes or such that I could be in. I need to be here. Anyway, you look good. How do you feel?"

This woman made Bucky really nervous, more so than she already was.

"Are you a real nurse?" she asked.

"Goodness gracious, no!" said the woman. "I wouldn't know what I was doing or where to begin. No, I'm the voice you heard from the well. The one who told you to go home."

Now Clement was more engaged in the conversation.

"I heard you too," he added.

"Oh good, that means I was loud enough." She took a long look at Clement. "You look familiar to me. Do I know you?"

Clement was shocked. He had never met this woman before in his life other than when she let him into the room a while ago, and he'd remember her if he had otherwise.

"I think not," was all he could come up with.

"Oh. Well, as long as you are both all right." She turned to leave. "I'll be watching you."

Bucky gasped again.

"I mean," said the beautiful nurse in white, "I'll be watching OVER you; I think that's the appropriate term." She looked confused again and then left the room.

Bucky was sitting up straight now and more eager to go home than she had ever been when in the hospital before, and that was to have her tonsils out when she was five.

"I don't trust her."

Clement's eyes were all starry. "I think she's beautiful."

"She's not that beautiful. And I still don't trust her. Now what were you saying?"

Clement cleared his throat. "The kids were all going to throw me in the well. I persuaded them not to and to attack Potty instead. So, I really should be down there, not him."

The door flew open and almost hit Clement in the face. The beautiful nurse came rushing in, looking all excited.

"What did you say?" She pulled the door away from Clement's almost smashed up nose. He got up from his chair and sat down on the empty bed to see the nurse better.

"Sorry, young man, but what did you say?"

Clement repeated himself, rather embarrassed.

"Tell me, do you have asthma?"

Clement looked surprised. The nurse was looking at him so intently, as if her life depended on it.

"A little, why?"

The nurse heaved a sigh and started to laugh.

"Oh, good. That's good. For a moment there..."

Clement was now getting a little offended. "Now see here," he started, "what could be good about that?"

"It means," said the nurse, "that I was right all along. And so are you. You should be."

"I should be right?"

"You should be in the well. Instead of Potty."

"Peter!" interjected Bucky.

"Peter. You should have been there instead of Peter. But what's done is done, and I'm not going to get in trouble for someone else's mistake. Anyway, I'm glad you're both here, and we can start bright and early in the morning."

Bucky had had enough. She hit the bed with her fist and nearly screamed. Her mother, apparently, didn't hear any of this but kept announcing the winning lotto numbers in a hushed whisper.

"Get ready for what?" demanded Bucky.

"Why, to save the world, dear. Why do you think I'm here in the hospital? For my health? Now get some sleep. Both of you."

Then she smiled, turned to Clement and patted him on his hat covered head, smiled again and left the room, almost skipping.

In a wink she was back, all smiles and unnervingly happy.

"I just found out," she said, "that a certain toothpaste company has gone pro-health. I'm so happy! I bet when they were anti-health it was just horrible. You should use it."

Then she skipped back out.

Clement took one look at Bucky and whistled. "That's one strange nurse."

FIRST ORDER OF BUSINESS

Peter found himself in the most interesting and curious kitchen he had ever seen. It wasn't like Grandma Nesbitt's by a long shot. It was carved out of the bowl of a tree and loaded with every possible fruit you could think of hanging from the ceiling, if you could call it that. Yet, despite all the fruit, the strongest and most delightful scent was that of apple cider and cinnamon in the kitchen, and bacon frying and chocolate baking in the oven. The way into this kitchen, from the top deck of the floating forest, was through a door in the first "mast" or tree that Peter saw. The foremast, of course, but to Peter it was still a pine tree. Ray the Taller walked up to it, found a knob of bark, turned it, and a door opened. The door also had a small window, but you couldn't tell that was what it was until you were on the inside looking out. They walked in and down a small and narrow staircase, like a ladder, into the galley. Here was where all the delicious smells were located, in the heart of a pine tree. Peter looked about him and here and there were bowls, plates, cutting things, forks, knives, spoons, all made of wood.

"Don't tell me," Peter said to Ray the Taller, "you're elves, and you make cookies."

"I'm not an elf, and my wife bakes the cookies."

Ray the Shorter chuckled.

"I eat the cookies and no."

Peter looked at him. He was smiling ear to ear, his spectacles pushed up on the bridge of his nose.

"No what?"

"I'm not an elf. Although I'd like to meet one someday."

From an unnoticed pantry door in the back of the inside of the fantastic tree kitchen (that also led to the lower decks) came two elderly women dressed in old fashioned peasant clothes, talking amongst themselves about how to effectively flavor a certain apple dessert with just enough vanilla to send the person eating the pastry into new levels of delight. Peter wanted to try the stuff immediately.

Ray the Shorter spoke up.

"Ah, Peter, these are our wives. This is my wife, Novali, who is quite unlike me in stature," and that was true; she looked to be six foot one if anything and as skinny as a rail, "and this here is Ray's wife Durice. She looks more like me." He pronounced Durice like "Dyur iss see."

"That's because," said Durice, "I'm his sister. You could say I married Ray and Ray's sister Novali married my brother. And you'd be right. Now, Ray was telling us he was picking someone up at Far Rock. Would that be you?"

Peter looked at Durice, a small and plump gray-haired lovely with spectacles like her brother. "I don't know the names of your land, but that could very well be it."

Ray the Taller piped in, "We're always looking for someone to help out. There is usually someone there, and at other points we like to visit, who need to get to somewhere else. It's how we make a little money in our retirement."

Peter thought for a moment. This was quite an extraordinary hallucination. The detail was staggering.

"All right, I'm going to ask."

Everyone stopped what they were doing or saying and turned to look at Peter. There was an awkward silence for a beat or two.

"What," he began, "did you do for a living?"

Ray the Shorter jumped in on this one. "Glad you asked, dear boy! Glad you asked. I'm a story teller."

"And I'm a puppeteer," said Ray the Taller. "Together we would put on the most delightful shows. You really must not be from around here if you haven't heard of," and he got all theatrical, "Ray and Ray!"

Peter applauded. This sounded wonderful. What an incredible coma he was enjoying.

"Would you like to see the puppets?" asked Durice.

"Oh yes, I really would."

Ray the Taller feigned humility and feigned it well. "Oh no, don't bore the poor lad. I'm sure he wouldn't want to see the famous puppets. The most famous puppets in all of Innerworld."

Peter laughed. Of course, he would. He stretched a bit and a sleeve on his sweater started to pull apart.

"Really, Peter," said Novali, "you really should get clothes more for your age. I have something down in the hold that might fit you," and she disappeared out the back doorway. By this time Ray the Taller had eagerly pulled out from behind a table a large wooden trunk. Ray the Shorter had cleared the very same table of dishes and utensils and had spread a cloth over the top. Ray the Taller opened the trunk and very carefully handed a couple of cloth wrapped objects to the other Ray. These were unwrapped and two fantastic looking figures of a man and a giant monstrosity were placed standing up on the table.

"Now," said Ray the Taller, "watch closely but remember it has been sometime and I may be rusty." So, he just stood there. He did nothing but stand at the table and stare at the puppets. Nothing happened. For another beat, moment or what seemed like a full ten minutes there was silence and nothing happened. Then, nothing. Then there was something. The figures began to move.

Peter was wide-eyed. This was incredible. There were no strings, no rods or wires or anything that he could see. Ray the Taller just stood at the table's edge, arms folded, looking very intently at the two figures, which were chasing each other around the table.

Peter was awestruck.

"What do you think?" asked Ray the Shorter with a huge grin on his face, and his eyes all sparkly behind those spectacles, "Aren't they well made?"

Peter wasn't quite sure what to say at all. He finally, after clearing his throat, came up with something that sounded too pretentious.

"The verisimilitude is astounding."

"What?" said Ray the Taller, and when he did the two puppets fell lifeless to the table, as if they had been dropped.

"It's a word I learned in school. It means they're very life-like."

"Ah ha!" yelled Ray the Shorter, clapping his hands, "I told you, you still have it! Well done my friend!"

Novali came up from the hold carrying some clothes. She handed them to Peter while Durice held open the pantry door.

"There's plenty of room in here to change. Fifteen years old and no decent clothes or shoes."

Peter looked at her quizzically. "I'm twelve."

They all laughed. Peter went into the pantry, which was very large and smelled of bread and had another stairwell that obviously led down to the sleeping quarters. He changed his clothes. When he came out, he was looking a lot more comfortable, even though the peasant shirt was a little too large, and the moccasins were just a little too wide.

"At the rate you're growing," said Durice, "those clothes won't last a year."

Peter thanked them and started looking around the galley.

"I owe you all some toast."

They all laughed with delight.

"But I don't see the toaster."

This also was very funny. Durice got up and brought a loaf of fresh bread over to the table near the starboard side of the galley where there was also access to a spit with some warm coals under it.

"If by toaster you mean this, we have one."

Peter shrugged and walked over to the spit and started slicing bread. He did have a talent for toast, because he knew just when to take a slice off the spit. So, after everyone had two or three slices of fresh baked bread toast with creamy butter and honey, Peter asked the obvious.

"How did you do it?" He was looking at Ray the Taller.

"You mean the puppets? Talent dear boy and practice. I told you I was a little rusty."

"You see," began the other Ray, "we love to tell stories about the northern land of Obloomn, but everyone has been there, and giant schlurrgs are really not very interesting anymore, so we retired."

"We want to travel all of Innerworld and find that portal."

Peter nearly dropped his toast.

"What portal?" He was sure this had to do with the well he had fallen down.

"Oh, I don't really know. There's an old legend I was told as a boy about a portal to another world. I just can't help but believe there is something more to life than what we can see and smell. Really, wouldn't it be wonderful if there were other worlds? Fantastic worlds with strange creatures and interesting heroes and dangerous quests? I think it is all a dream, but something inside me says that it just might really be."

Durice looked at Peter who was very pale.

"Are you all right, son?"

"Yep. Fine." He closed his mouth tight.

Ray the Shorter was very excited. "So, we came from Folsborn, which is of course, every schoolboy knows, the source of this marvelous ocean. And in our dotage, we felt, what the hey, let's see if there are other dimensions and fantastic worlds. I know it's just a fantasy, but I'm a story-teller, and I love a good fantasy." He looked a little confused, "By the way, you never told us where you're from."

Peter choked down his piece of toast. "Surprisingly," he started, "you're in luck."

THEY COME WHEN IT RAINS

Slap, slap, slap, scrape. Slap, slap, squeak, scrape, slap. Slap, squeak, squeak, scrape, thump.

"This car needs new wiper blades."

"What was that, Bev, dear?"

Bucky sat in the torn and tortured leather of the back seat of an old Chrysler that smelled of stale smoke and peppered beef. That entire day had been one wrong thing after another. She woke up in the hospital, nervous that somehow that strange woman would be looking over her and smelling of medicine, but there was no one else in the room besides Clement and her mother. So, there she sat, waiting for the strange nurse who wasn't a nurse at all to arrive and to get her moving onto whatever crazy scheme she had planned.

That didn't happen. Bucky waited an hour without saying anything, and when she did, Clement nearly jumped out of his seat. Bucky's mom just yawned and commented on how wonderful the news had been.

So, it was time to leave the hospital and still no strange nurse. Bucky was starting to feel it might have been a dream but Clement was with her and he also had been expecting the nurse to show up, but not with the same sense of dread that Bucky had.

By the time they had made it to the parking lot, her mom noticed something was wrong with their car. It wasn't there. Apparently, it had been towed away because Bucky's mom had parked in a space reserved for doctors needed during emergencies. Time to find another car home and no breakfast either.

It started to rain.

That was this morning and now here she was, in a very different smelling car from the one she was used to. Clement was sitting next to her, looking very sullen. It was raining hard and Bucky could see that that made him feel more miserable than he had a few hours before, like all the world was spitting at him. Bucky thought she'd try to say something cheerful, but all she got out of her head was, "Raining, huh?"

Clement moaned and sat back.

Bucky's mother, who always called her Bev since her real name was Beverly, was sitting in the front seat. She shifted a bit and repeated herself.

"What was that you said, Bev?"

"This car needs new windshield wipers."

"Make a note."

Make a note was what Bucky's mother always said when she didn't have an answer for any question or statement as in, "This car needs new windshield wipers" or "This car needs new brakes" or "Maybe you shouldn't watch the news so much" and so on. Bucky never made a note, but she did seem to always remember when it was necessary.

Bucky's mom turned her head to look a little ways into the back of the car.

"So, Potty, how are you doing?"

Bucky looked at Clement and then corrected her mother, ever so respectfully.

"This is my other friend." At that Clement seemed to smile a bit. "His name is Clement. Potty's name is really Peter." Her mother was silent for a moment.

"Well, whatever, I'm glad you're out of that nasty refrigerator or whatever they found you in. And that little rat of a horrid boy that threw you into it should get thirty years, or the death penalty if you ask me."

Now Clement frowned again.

"I'm not the one who was thrown anywhere, Mrs. Newcastle; that would be Potty."

"Peter," interrupted Bucky.

"Peter. And he fell; no, that's not altogether true, he was 'thrown' down a well."

"Oh, good heavens!" laughed Bucky's mom. "No one has gotten thrown down a well since, oh, Joseph."

Clement just sat back and frowned. Bucky could hear him muttering under his breath, "I hate the rain. I hate it when people didn't believe me and I hate how I feel right now."

Bucky wanted to console him, but before she could say anything her mother started talking again.

"So, Clement, who exactly are you? I mean, in relation to all these friends of my daughter's?"

"I'm the little rat boy who should get thirty years or death." Then he started to cry.

There was a blaring of a horn, a screech of burning rubber tires and the car sluiced around on a cushion of water as it, seemingly on its own, tried to dodge an object running across the flooded street.

"Good golly!" screamed Bucky's mom. "What was that? A dog?"

"I didn't see anything," said Bucky, as she strained her neck to peek out the window on Clement's side of the car, for that was the direction her mother was looking.

"It looked like a rodent or a dog or a lizard, but it was big, too big to be a lizard, and no tail," said Bucky's mom.

Clement, who had suddenly stopped crying, just gave Bucky a silent look of recognition. Bucky swallowed and turned around in her seat. She wanted to cry but couldn't.

The car adjusted to the sudden movement and everything was smooth again. The rain pelted the windshield even harder. The noise was a little frightening and so was the fact that a person couldn't really see out the front as far as the edge of the hood of the engine. Bucky squirmed.

"We really should have a different car."

"Don't tell me," countered Bucky's mom. "I'm not driving."

The cab driver looked back over his greasy coat covered shoulder at Bucky. "I've been saying that for years, but who listens?" Then he turned back to the task of driving in the most horrific rain storm that Bucky could remember being out in.

There was a sudden thump under the car.

"Ugh!" screamed Bucky, "What was that?"

"One of those rat things I reckon," said the cabdriver. "Not a rat like you, young man," he made clear to Clement, "but like the ones that are swarming all over the car and street."

It was true. Through the watery windshield Bucky could vaguely see shapes of short, squat evil-looking vermin or reptiles (she couldn't make up her mind) with bright red eyes, jumping on and off the hood of the cab as the cabdriver tried to maneuver in and around the giant gushes of rain and pot holes in the streets and herds or flocks or whatever one called them, of the strange tailless rat-like lizard things.

"I'm going to pull over."

"Oh, no you're not!" yelled Bucky. "Not while they're out there. They could get us."

"Make a note," said Bucky's mom. Bucky squealed and hid her head in her hands with her eyes squeezed tight. Clement just looked on in horror.

The cabdriver tried valiantly to not spin out or "hydroplane" as he said the hip kids in town called it, but he did it again anyway and the car went spinning out of control.

For two eternally long seconds, maybe five, Bucky's whole twelve years flashed before her eyes. She saw herself as a small child, blowing out the flame on one candle on a white birthday cake. She saw her mother, long ago it seemed, standing at the doorway of their old house, shocked that her lottery ticket wasn't the winning one, and all her hopes for a future as a television newscaster seemed to her to be dashed. Apparently, Bucky's mom felt she had to win the lottery and get a whole new wardrobe and hair style and everything a newscaster would need before she could go to newscasting school, which also cost large amounts of money.

Then her mother started watching too much TV; it was like she was hooked and wouldn't move. There were times she couldn't even get off the couch she was so intrigued with the news programs. Bucky had to learn to cook and clean for the two of them and to make sure her mother stood up and let the blood flow to her feet. The roles had changed and Bucky was now the mom, it seemed.

This all happened in a flash, then in a furry of screeching tires and shattering glass, the car flipped onto its side and came to a crashing halt in the now rushing river of a street somewhere several blocks from home.

Thank goodness all of them had their seatbelts on. Bucky, who sat behind the cabdriver, was on the side of the car that was up in the air and her mom and Clement were on the side that started filling with water, for the windows had cracked and split open. On the window at Bucky's side there was a rat lizard, looking in with a toothy grin and getting pelted by all the bullet-like rain, as if it were happy, they were in such a situation.

The engine had shut off automatically and the cabdriver immediately cried out, "Everybody all right?"

"There's water coming in Mom's window and Clement's!" Bucky yelled back.

The cabdriver tried to reach Bucky's mom, but couldn't while he was strapped in. So, holding onto the door handle on his left, he pressed the release button of his safety belt with his right hand and then reached for Bucky's mom. Grabbing her hand, he started to pull her toward him, but she was stuck in her own belt and the water was starting to rush in. Bucky could tell it was cold. Her mother was coughing and spitting and trying hard to get loose and with a final effort she was free.

Bucky did the same for Clement and he was soaked but out of his strap. Now was the moment where they had to decide how to get out, for there were several lizard rats all over the car, on top and the side, as well as out on the street and floating in the water, and the rain was punishing the ground with large and heavy drops of cold water.

Feeling that Bucky's mom and the two kids were unharmed, the cabdriver pushed his driver side door up and over, throwing three rat lizards into the river-like street. Several more jumped up onto his arm and shoulder as he pushed and pulled his way out of the car. They didn't bite, but they felt awfully dangerous, like there was some sort of disease about them; the same way you might feel if you had a hoard of cockroaches crawling all over your arm. He just shook them off and kept on climbing out of the car. The wind was blowing hard, making it seem like he was about to inhale pints of water. He made it out onto his side of the car, and then pulled Bucky's mom up and told her to stand in the car while he got the kids out. She could help push if need be.

That was how it was done. Once Bucky's door was open, the cabdriver grabbed her hand and her mom helped push her and Clement (who was holding onto Bucky's other hand) out while the cabdriver pulled along with one arm and fought off lizard rats with the other.

Oh, the rain was cold, the wind was harsh, the water in the street was deep and they all managed to get off the car and soak their shoes and pants up to the knees. Wading through the fast-rushing water and almost slipping, Bucky and Clement made it to the sidewalk, only slightly less intimidating than the street, and the cabdriver and Bucky's mom came right up along with them.

"How far are you from home?" yelled the cabdriver, because the wind and rain made it hard to hear. He was staring at the overturned cab. It was swarming with the lizard rats. None of the creatures seemed to be bothering them at the moment; they were only interested in the car. He could see them tearing up the upholstery with their little monkey-like hands, pulling out wires from under the dash and searching through the glove compartment as if they were looking for something important. All that did was leave a mess of torn paper all over the front seat and broken windows.

"We're just about there, I think," yelled back Bucky's mom.

"No Mom, we're at least three blocks from home. We'll never get there if they try to get us."

"I'll protect you," said the cabdriver, and he meant it. He looked around, and found they were standing in front of a house that had a sprinkler key rod on the porch.

"I'm sure whoever lives here will let me borrow this," said the cabdriver and he ran up and got the sprinkler key, which was not like a normal key, but was about three feet long made of metal with a handle shaped like a triangle on one end and dangerous looking prongs, two of them, on the other end. Certainly, he could use it to fight off lizard rats if he had to.

So, he was well armed and they were all determined to get back to Bucky's home. How Clement was then going to get home no one knew, but Bucky offered to let him stay at her house.

"In fact," said her mother, "we're all going to stay there, with the fire on and hot food on the stove." This made everyone more determined so they set out in search of the Newcastle house and for the first time since Bucky could remember, her mother made it very clear that Bucky was in charge.

Off they went, Bucky in the lead, through all kinds of puddles and wet grass and crossing dangerously wet streets, streaming with dirty, oily water and always looking over their shoulders to make sure no lizard monkey rats were following them. Several times Bucky's mother or Clement would lose their footing, but the cabdriver was quick to catch them and made sure no one got too wet. As they neared the street Bucky lived on, her mom and the cabdriver were now holding onto each other, as if her mom had tried on purpose to fall into the muddy flooded streets, and Bucky knew for the first time that she was feeling better and taking an interest in other people. That wasn't going to last, however, because of what happened next.

As Bucky and Clement turned the corner onto the actual street where Bucky's house lived, just a few houses away, Bucky looked behind her and tried to scream a loud scream but was too scared to make a noise. Coming from behind the cabdriver and Bucky's mom was a mass of dark, beady red-eyed lizard monkey rats slowly following, like stalking cats, hundreds of them. Maybe thousands.

Bucky couldn't say anything, but she could point and so she did. Bucky's mom turned around to see what Bucky was pointing at. Clement had stopped as well, and looked in the same direction. As the cabdriver also turned, Bucky finally was able to say something and said the first sensible thing she could think of.

"Run."

They did. Without hesitation, splashing and slipping in the street, with the heavy rain crashing down upon them, they ran. They ran, fell, slipped, got up and ran again, a whirlwind of hands and shoes, purses and sprinkler keys, boys and girls all muddy and skinned knee'd, they made it to Bucky's porch. One would think the relief of making it home would be the first emotion they would have felt, but what they saw sitting on Bucky's porch right in front of the door made Bucky scream, and the rest stop short as if stunned by a flying brick.

"They come when it rains," said the Beautiful Woman, sitting there, all dressed in muddy white.

THE QUEST

Peter had finished relating everything that had happened to him in the last two days, although it had seemed like months, including his meeting with the mysterious Beautiful Woman all Dressed in White. He also included details about his home, his best friend Bev or Bucky as everyone else called her. He spoke of his Grandma Nesbitt and how she loved him and took care of him after his mom and dad had died, and all the stuff and things of everyday life that he took for granted and really missed. Things like his computer, his television and his cell phone. The two Rays and their wives just sat there at the table, speechless.

As Peter had noticed before there was a porthole in the door to the galley and Peter could see through it enough to tell it was getting late. The sky was a dark blue-gray, at least, what he could see of it.

Ray the Taller tried to say something, but was having a bit of trouble. Ray the Shorter was just dumbfounded. He stared ahead, as if looking far off into the distance, and then a pleasant smile started to form around his face until it reached his ears and parted his ample mouth in one, big, guffaw.

"I was right!"

"You were right," encouraged Ray the Taller.

Novali and Durice were silent. They were looking at each other, and it was really hard for Peter to tell what they were thinking. Not that it mattered, for they weren't real anyway, he thought.

"Well, there you have it. I'm from another world, if I'm from anywhere. You don't believe me?"

"Its clear Ray does," said Ray the Taller.

"Yes, I think it must be true."

"Well," said Peter, "that's rather trusting. Here I am, a stranger, whom you picked up on a whim, who has told you a most remarkable tale and you readily believe me."

"As I see it, young man," said Ray the Taller, "there are three ways of looking at this. Either you are lying or you are mad or you're telling the truth."

Peter remembered this argument from a book he had read about a similar alternate world. Clearly that would have been from Peter's subconscious; it all made sense. [1]

"Or," Peter countered, "it could mean that I'm sick, lying in a coma at the bottom of a well or in a hospital, or in the morgue for all I know."

"That's not likely, son," said Durice, "we've been around a long time without you."

"No!" This was the last straw. If Peter was going to go mad, he wasn't going to go without a fight. "There are no magical worlds, or portals, no! There is nothing beyond the natural world! If I can't see it, smell it, or feel it--" and at that he slammed his fist into the table where he was sitting and it hurt.

"Ouch!" he cried, "I mean, scientifically, of course, then it isn't real! A wise man in my world, ugh! My world! Whatever! A wise man I once read asked, 'Isn't it enough to look at a garden and accept its beauty without believing there are fairies at the bottom?' He was wise." [2]

"No," said Ray the Taller, "it's not enough to see a garden and appreciate its beauty without acknowledging the skill and artistry of the gardener. You don't always get to see him, but you see his handiwork."

"And," added Ray the Shorter, "some of my best friends are fairies and they are quite pleasant people."

This really disturbed Peter. He couldn't take this kind of logic because it was beginning to seduce him into thinking the impossible, or highly improbable could be real. That was too much for him. He got up from where he was sitting and headed for the door.

"Where are you going?" asked Novali.

"I need some air. I need to figure out what to do next. I need to be alone for a minute."

He opened the door and went outside, where it was really starting to get cold and dark.

After wandering around the ship for a minute he found a soft, mossy hillock on which to sit and contemplate the confusing universe he either just found himself in, or had been in all along.

It took maybe ten minutes but Ray the Shorter came looking for him.

"Don't get up, Peter. Stay there. I'm not going to be here long. I just wanted to make sure you were all right and to let you know the wind is up."

---

[1] The Chronicles of Narnia, see end notes.
[2] Douglas Adams, see end notes.

It was. There was a strong sea breeze blowing over the bow and Peter could feel it in his hair, which was uncommonly long for only a few days since his last visit to the barber.

"We should go in," said Ray.

"I guess you're right. I just needed a moment."

"Of course, you can still have it. Just don't take too long."

Ray still stood, looking down at Peter. It was clear he had more to say.

"What did you mean earlier?"

"About what?"

Ray smiled. He sat next to Peter and touched Peter's shoulder.

"What you said about not knowing what to do next."

Peter grimaced. "I didn't quite tell you everything. The Beautiful Woman All Dressed in White gave me a quest."

"Really?" Ray the Shorter was delighted. "Really now! She did that? What quest?"

"I have to go somewhere and stop someone, and I don't know how to do it. I have to find three magical somethings and empty them. I don't even know what to look for."

Ray looked a little sullen.

"Oh. I see. I now can tell a little why you are so confused. You don't have all the answers. Well, neither do I, my lad. Neither do I. Where are you supposed to go?"

Peter shrugged. "I don't know, someplace across the sea." He waved in a general direction over his head. "I think she said Covenswold."

There was a loud intake of air and it was Ray the Shorter who inhaled, and sharply. He took off his spectacles and rubbed his eyes, then his forehead. He dropped his spectacles into the moss and started digging around for them. Peter reached down and picked them up right away and handed them back to Ray the Shorter.

"Is that bad?" asked Peter.

"Oh yes. Oh yes, son. It's bad. We, that is, I, or we, ah! It can't be done. We can't take you there. We just can't."

The wind picked up and the sea was choppy. Peter looked up at the night sky, but there was no moon or stars that he could see, just a faint and fuzzy round glow that could be a moon if it wanted to, but was either too tired or no moon at all.

It was a dark, cloudy sea he was lost on, with what seemed like a frightened little man at his side, and no one visibly steering the vessel. Peter felt really lost.

"What do I do?" He really was imploring. If you can ask anyone for help, you should be able to ask an adult, even if he was a coma induced delusion of an adult, he must know more than Peter knew.

"Clear your mind."

"What?"

"Clear your mind, renew your mind really, young man. You must. This person I think you are going to have to encounter is not friendly to strangers from other lands, that is for sure. At least, not in reality. Oh, he appears to be kind and wise, but he is cunning, oh, so cunning. Clear your mind. He will try to corrupt it, confuse it with logic that really isn't logic at all. If you renew it daily, and think on wonderful things, you have a chance."

Peter looked very frightened.

"I understand. You're scared and alone," said Ray, "and it is true I can't go with you."

"The adults always abandon the kids." Peter held back a tear.

"No, it's not like that. We're wanted men, Ray and I. We're not retired, we're not on a pleasure cruise. We made that up. We probably shouldn't have, but we did. We're running for our lives, Peter. We've broken his most important law. We chose to believe in that which we cannot see."

"You are," Peter asked, "speaking of Politicus Mediosus?"

"Oh, the very same. A wicked, vengeful spirit of a fallen man. And yet, the people of Covenswold follow him, blindly it seems. Nothing he says is doubted. Nothing he does is wrong, weak or even a simple human mistake in their minds."

Peter wanted to change the subject. "How do I renew my mind?"

"Clear it."

"In my world, there are people who spend their whole lives trying to do that, to have absence of thought, even for a second," said Peter, thoughtfully.

"Well, I don't know if that works; certainly not in my experience, but I'm not wise in the ways of your people. What I do is think on wonderful things, beautiful things. I think on things that are good to tell, that help and heal people in their hearts, their minds. I think on these things, and fill my thoughts with what I know is truth. But I have to empty it of lies. Empty your mind, Peter, and fill it with loving thoughts. Love is what I think of. How to use it, how to give it, so that others are better off. Never used to be that way. I'm old now, and maybe a little nutty. I was banished for it. Me and my family. Here we are, adrift, on a boat that is completely capable of making its own decisions. Fortunately for us, it is sympathetic to our cause."

"Ah. A magic boat. I should have guessed."

"No," countered Ray, "not magic. It is an organic, living being. It grows, it eats, it sleeps. It is."

"There is no magic in my world."

Ray laughed. This was rich to him because the story Peter had related earlier about his world belied that very notion.

"Ha! A world where, what do you call them? Smart phones can tell you where you are, show you the faces of your friends, tell you when it rains, the time of day, oh. And tell stories! Books and shows! And it fits in the palm of your hand? If I didn't have a renewed mind, I'd say you were a horrid liar. But you're not, are you, Peter? Are you a liar?"

"No sir," said Peter, "I love truth. I just don't know if I like truth. It is, to say the least, like trying to grasp a thin thread with a giant hand."

Ray smiled again. "Your world has a kind of magic, Peter, even though you don't see it. It is wonder and grace, if what you say about your friend and family is true. Things I wish we had more of here, in Innerworld. So, don't be too long in emptying your mind and filling it with good and healthy things." Ray got up and started up toward the bow. "The wind is up. We may be in for it."

In a wisp he was gone, and Peter was alone with his thoughts.

"How does one empty his own mind?" he asked himself. "Think on wonderful things." So, Peter remembered Bucky, and how kind she was to him. He thought of Grandma Nesbitt, and how she took him in and became a second mother to him. He thought of the Beautiful Woman All Dressed in White and remembered how she fed him, and placed a tremendous amount of trust in him. Even if she was a figment of his imagination, then that must mean he needed to trust himself, trust the gnawing feeling in his gut that there was more to life than cause and effect. Before he knew it, he felt better, but it started to rain and he was getting too wet.

As he got up to go to the galley cabin, he caught out of the corner of his eye what looked like two little red eyes staring at him through the bushes in the center of the ship. Peter quickly looked in the direction he thought they were but there was nothing there.

In the galley, there was food cooking. This was Peter's third night since falling in the well, and his second night in Innerworld, or the hospital if that were the case, but he decided the food was real enough, because he was hungry and it smelled so wonderfully delicious. Onion and carrots, roast beef and hot cider. The galley was simply swimming in wonderful smells.

"Ray?" asked Peter.

Both Rays turned and looked at him and said together, "What?"

"Is it OK with you if I think on these smells?"

THE PURPOSE

The cabdriver, brandishing his procured sprinkler key, turned to see if he had to clobber some lizard monkey rats, but they just stood across the street, a few hundred or so, and watched, silently.

Clement was the first to speak. "Maybe we should get inside?"

That seemed like a great idea to everyone else. They stood in front of The Beautiful Woman All Dressed in Mud and she just stared back.

"Oh!" She realized. "I'm in the way." She stood up and apologized. Bucky's mom immediately took out her house key from her rain-damaged purse and dropped it in the grass. The cabdriver got on his knees and soaked them while digging around for the key. Bucky had her own and in seconds had the door open.

The inside of the house had a warm and cozy feeling, because Bucky's mom forgot to turn the heat off, and it was a good thing, not that she forgot, (because as you know, you should never forget such a thing) but that it was warm and cozy inside. A minute later and all were standing, dripping wet in the tiny foyer of Bucky's house. The lizard rat monsters were still across the street, watching with what looked like only academic interest, which made them all the more frightening.

"I'll start the tea," said Bucky's mom, and into the kitchen she went.

"I'll help," said the cabdriver, whose name happened to be Bert. He then went into the kitchen which was just the opposite side of the house as the den and back porch.

Clement and Bucky took off their coats and hung them up on the coat rack in the foyer and headed toward the den. The Beautiful Woman followed close behind.

Bucky started a fire in the gas fireplace and sat down on the sofa. Clement sat next to her and the Beautiful Woman just stood there.

"Does my dress look like a bell when I turn around really fast?"

asked the Beautiful Woman, who then turned in place several times rather fast, splashing mud all over the den walls, Bucky's chair, Bucky's mom's chair, the TV, the sofa and Clement and Bucky.

"No," said Bucky, "the mud keeps it pretty straight."

The Beautiful Woman looked disappointed. "Oh."

"Sit down, please," said Bucky.

The Beautiful Woman looked very happy and sat rather hard and floppily into the mud splattered chair that Bucky's mom usually sat in.

"Comfy!" she exclaimed.

"Yeah, that's my mom's. The one next to it is mine, if you want to sit there..."

"No, this is quite comfortable. Thank you."

Bucky frowned. How was she going to get The Beautiful Woman out of her mother's chair without being rude? The Beautiful Woman just sat there, with a rather unnerving smile on her face, as if she was waiting for the server in a restaurant to take her order.

"Can I get you anything?" Bucky asked.

"Tea."

"My mom is getting the tea."

"Oh," and she just kept staring and smiling. Once in a long while she would blink.

"I don't think," began Bucky, "that I ever caught your name."

"I am the Beautiful Woman All Dressed in White!" she said with a lilt of a laugh.

"Not anymore," offered Clement.

"Mud is fun."

"Yes," began Bucky, again, "that's all well and good, but who, exactly," and she motioned her hands toward the Beautiful Woman, "is the Beautiful Woman All Dressed in White?"

"Me!" she sang, and at that, stood up on her tip toes, and spun around once more, splattering anew the furniture and carpet with wet, brown mud. Clement wiped some mud out of his eye and suggested the Beautiful Woman stay seated until she was good and dry.

"Oh yes! And warm with tea! Can't wait!"

Bucky was not going to give up. She forged ahead.

"Beautiful Woman All Dressed in White," she started, again.

"Yes?"

"Why are you here?"

The Beautiful Woman wrinkled her brow as if trying to do a tax form by memory. The rain kept splattering the den windows. All Bucky and Clement could see outside was gray and damp with drops on the window. However, in the distance, they could still see a myriad of shining red eyes.

"I guess I didn't tell you yesterday," the Beautiful Woman finally said after what seemed like an hour, but was only a few seconds.

"No," said Bucky, "no you didn't."

The Beautiful Woman made herself more comfortable and smoothed out her muddy dress and wiped her hands on the arm rests of the chair, smiled and started to tell a tale so strange, so improbable that with all that had happened to her in the past three days, Bucky decided to believe it.

"I'm here to stop an eventual apocalypse that's not supposed to happen yet. And it's been a blast!"

Just then, Mrs. Newcastle and Bert came in with a tray of hot, steaming tea and a plate of mouth-watering chocolate chip cookies. Mrs. Newcastle set some cups on the coffee table in-between the children and the Beautiful Woman and poured the tea. Bert set down the plate of cookies, but not before taking a couple for himself. He bit into one and it was just the right kind of crunchy.

The Beautiful Woman's face lit up as she watched Bert eat his cookie. She hadn't realized just how hungry she was and the treats looked so tempting she took a cookie and ate it greedily. Oh! It was unlike anything she had eaten in this world before. It was crunchy, yet it had deliciously soft chocolate throughout. Thoroughly delightful they were, and she had two or three more.

"These are fantastic," she exclaimed, "what do you call them?"

Bucky looked incredulous. "Cookies."

At that, the Beautiful Woman's face changed dramatically. She looked like she just had been told she was eating a kitten. Spitting out the cookie crumbs and partially chewed chocolate bits all over the carpet she started to scream. With her muddy gloved hand, she tried to brush her tongue clean.

"What the heck?" It was Clement's turn to look incredulous.

The Beautiful Woman looked up, stunned.

"What did you call these?"

"Cookies," said Bucky, looking worried and slightly disgusted.

"Not spelled k-u-k-y-z?"

"No," replied Bucky, "spelled c-o-o-k-i-e-s."

"Oh, good. Because those things outside are called kukyz in Innerworld. I would never want to eat one of those. You don't know where they've been."

Bucky threw up her hands. "I give up. What are kukyz?"

The Beautiful Woman picked up the remains of her cookies and wrapped them up in a paper napkin that the exasperated Bert, who stood there, watching in horror, had left on the table. Bucky's mom was about to go get the vacuum. The Beautiful Woman, however, captured their attention right away.

"They are monsters. They were created by a deranged mind. All they do is follow you around, watch what you're doing, and report back to the mad man who made them. They sometimes stay with you, and you can never get rid of them. While you sleep, they watch you, wait until you forget they are there and then try to sell you something. Absolutely horrendous."

Bucky's mom went and got the vacuum anyway.

"I'm here to save both Innerworld and your world. What I call Outerworld. Peter is in Innerworld, where Clement was supposed to go, but missed it. Now it's up to Peter to stop that horrible Politikos Mediosus and set the worlds right again. He's mad, you know. He wants to come into this world and take over. He is mad with power.

"Why does Peter or Clement need to go?" asked Bert, who was really starting to believe it all.

"Politikos is originally from this world, so one of his kind must stop him. It is Peter's destiny, his purpose."

"So," started Clement, "I missed my purpose in life? Is that what you're saying, sitting there with mud and crumbs all over you?"

The Beautiful Woman wrinkled up her nose and looked to the ceiling. She shook her head.

"Not your purpose in life," she stated, "but a purpose that could have been yours and now is his."

Bert thought he'd have another cookie.

"Well, at least those animals outside can't get in."

"Not while I'm here," said the Beautiful Woman, "They know I'll smoosh 'em," and she did a grinding motion with her foot.

Mrs. Newcastle came back into the den with an upright vacuum and was searching for an outlet when she stopped for a minute and looked right at the Beautiful Woman.

"How can we help?" asked Bucky's mom. Bucky could have jumped out of orbit over this. Finally, her mother was getting involved in something. Then a weird look came over her mother's face, and she kept staring at the Beautiful Woman.

"What is it, Mom?"

The Beautiful Woman stared back. She smiled. There was chocolate chip cookie in her teeth.

"Haven't I," and Mrs. Newcastle stopped talking for a second. Then she picked up where she left off. "Haven't I seen you in a fashion magazine before?"

"Yep!" said the Beautiful Woman, "That's when I was alive in this world, before my fatal, and somewhat embarrassing, modeling accident."

There was a thunder clap, a lightening flash, and Bert spit out his tea and dropped his handful of cookies.

A PARTING PARTY

The rain was tortuous, and loud, and wet. The sea was turning like Peter's stomach, all queasy and slippery-like. The clouds were low, dark and angry, with hints of dark green on what was thought to be the horizon. It was hard to tell since the horizon was often blocked out by giant waves of dangerous and relentless water.

Ray and Ray, Durice and Novali were huddled in the little galley, holding onto the table and trying to keep all the flatware from flying off and landing against the wall. Peter was standing on the small staircase, desperately trying to hold onto the handle of the galley door, and keeping it closed. The water just wanted to force itself in, but he wouldn't let it if he could. Still, he was really sea sick and needed to run to a bathroom somewhere. He hadn't felt this way the entire time he was experiencing this new world until now.

But it should be expected, he thought, what with a storm at sea.

"How much longer do we have to endure this?" he asked.

"Haven't a clue, young man," answered Ray the Taller, "this is our first storm at sea."

"I find that hard to believe, with you being on the run and all."

Ray the Taller looked at Ray the Shorter, who was just a little green in the face.

"Yeah, I told him. What do you want? He needs our help and maybe we need his." Ray the Shorter went on to explain why they should help Peter get to Covenswold but now it seemed like it really wouldn't matter; the storm was surely blowing the ship off course.

"How do you think Forrest is handling all the water?" asked Novali. She was, of course, referring to the living ship.

"Quite well, I expect," answered Durice. She was the calmest of everyone. Apparently in her youth she used to go fishing on a large boat with her father and knew about storms at sea.

Some water splashed through the door that Peter was holding shut, apparently not tight enough. It was just because he got a little tired in the arms, and now the whole cabin had an inch of water to wade through.

"Sorry," was all he could say.

"Not much you can do about it, lad," said Ray the Taller. "Hopefully this storm will abate as soon as there is daylight."

"Where is the crew?" asked Peter.

"No crew," said Ray the Shorter. "We're it. Forrest does all the rest." He patted the wall with affection.

"Oh, because I saw a creature on deck before the storm got really big, just as it started to rain."

Ray the Taller tried standing up, but his sea legs had left him. He sat back down although Ray the Shorter had tried supporting him. Durice and Novali just gasped.

"What kind of creature?" asked Ray the Taller when he was seated again.

"Well," started Peter, "it was like a small animal, about the size of what I would call a baby chimpanzee; a monkey or lizard or rat-like animal, only it had red eyes and an ugly, monstrous-looking face. I didn't want to call it that, because I was told not all things ugly are evil, and if it was a crew member, well, how rude!"

Ray the Shorter stood up this time, more successfully, although the ship kept pitching ever so strongly.

"No, these ugly things are certainly evil, if they're what we think they are."

"So," said Ray the Taller, "we've been found out."

"What?" Peter didn't understand a thing about what Ray was saying. If this indeed was a coma induced dream, Peter wished to heaven his subconscious would stop teasing and let him in on the joke.

"Mediosus," began Novali, "was developing an army of spies, to watch all of us and keep us in his sights at all times. How he does it I don't know, but these little wicked creatures will betray us to our ends for sure." She thought for a moment. "How many did you see?"

"Just the one," said Peter.

Durice nodded thoughtfully. "We all knew the risks. Don't worry, son, we're prepared."

Ray and Ray looked at each other.

"We should get the bludgeons out then," said Ray the Taller. He stood up with Ray the Shorter and started toward the inner door to the pantry when there was a great shake, lots of noise like the grinding of rock only ten times worse, and then a flood of water. Peter could hardly see when something hard hit him on the head and all went black.

When Peter awoke, all was still and silent. His ears were filled with water, and the floor to the galley cabin was wet and smelled like mold. He sat up. His head hurt, but there was no bump or cut, as far as he could feel, and his body didn't seem to be injured, although his joints ached to high heaven. He stood up, a bit shaky, but was able to keep his balance.

No one else was in the cabin, so they either went below through the entry in the pantry or they were on deck. He walked toward the pantry and opened the door and took a step inside. He cracked his head on the overhead wood beam, and that surprised him. Not only did it hurt, but he hadn't done that the day before. The beam must have fallen. It was obviously daytime since the sun was shining through the porthole window. He looked at the overhead beam in the bright daylight and it certainly seemed intact and solid.

He called out below but got no answer, so he headed for the cabin door. It was open, probably from when the water poured in and Peter lost consciousness. He sloshed up the stair case to go outside, scraping his head again on top of the doorway, and found the ship was not moving at all.

When his eyes adjusted to the bright sunlight, a sunlight after a storm, but still diffused by the high clouds that hid the roof of the immense cavern that was Innerworld, he could see that the ship had run aground. The bow was part way into a beachhead, and no one was in sight.

Peter walked to the edge of the bow and looked over. He could see human footprints in the sand and decided the others had taken to exploring their new territory, for Peter was convinced they were shipwrecked on an island out in the middle of this underground ocean.

The beach only went up so far and then suddenly stopped at what looked like a large pile of slate and clay and chalk rock all stacked a hundred feet high or more. It was certainly frightening to think if the tide had been higher, the ship might have crashed right into the side of what was obviously a cliff. Peter looked at his surroundings and noticed at the top of the cliff were pine trees, and some other similar kinds of trees were dotted about the area to the right and left of him, stretching out to sea on the top of similar rocks. It would have been beautiful and serene if it weren't for the fact the ship had run aground.

Peter wondered to himself how much damage the ship must have sustained. Then he had a peculiar shivering sensation down his spine, and felt as if someone was watching and he wasn't alone on the ship. He quickly turned around, expecting to see the ugly red-eyed creature, but there was nothing there. He gave it up to his obviously active imagination and looked for a way to climb off the ship.

He really wasn't that far up off the sand but he didn't want to risk jumping, not yet. He lowered himself over the edge and tried to find a foot-hold in the side of the ship with his feet. His water-soaked moccasins were too tight and his shins scraped on the edges of the ship. His pants had either shrunk or ridden up to his knees.

He decided to let go and then he landed with a thump. The sand was soft enough that he didn't really hurt himself, but it was a tad jarring. He stood up and looked around. He turned and looked out to sea. It seemed calm. It was hard to believe there was such a storm the night before.

He scratched his chin because it itched and found something rough and unfamiliar there. He thought it might be dried blood, or a scab or something from possibly hitting his face when he fell in the night after his head got hit, by what he didn't know. He tried to pull the dried blood off his chin but it wouldn't come off and it hurt. He didn't have a mirror so he felt his whole face and there were soft, prickly sticky things all over it, back to his ears and under his nose and under his chin, and down his neck.

"Good heavens!" he said aloud, "I've grown a beard."

Indeed, he had. In the three days he'd been in Innerworld, he had grown healthier, taller, and seemingly older. How old would he appear? He couldn't go back and look for a mirror because the sudden thought that his friends were here on land and maybe looking for him filled his mind and he decided to wait and look at himself later.

No time for vanity, he thought. He headed off in the direction the footprints were leading. He was suddenly very hungry and was angry with himself that he didn't bring anything to eat. Changing his mind again about going back to the ship, he turned around and noticed that the ship was not quite in the same position it had been when he leaped off. It almost looked like it had a pair of elbows and was resting what could be its chin in its hands, if it had any, and as far as Peter knew it hadn't.

"I'll eat later," he said aloud and turned back toward the task at hand, which was finding out what happened to Ray and Ray and Mrs. Ray and, well, the other Mrs. Ray.

It took him a few seconds to find the footprints and make out exactly where they were going, which was slightly to his left and up into the trees that crested that side of the cliff. He shrugged, took a deep breath and trundled on.

There was a loud grumbling or moaning sound behind him, and when he turned around, the ship was a little further up onto the sand.

"Tide is going out," he thought, "but how can there be a tide without a moon? Does Innerworld have a moon?" These were his thoughts as he headed onward.

Up the left side of the cliff edge there was a rough path through some underbrush. He decided, since it was at least a path, that perhaps this was where his new friends had come, or had gone, and taken the path, and he was right. Though the ground was harder, and the footprints fainter than on the sand, he at least could see something. So, he climbed the path and soon found himself on top of the cliff, looking out over the beach, where the ship was resting on its forearms.

There was something not quite right about that. Peter had to think for a bit and then it hit him like a rock in the back of the head.

"Ships don't have forearms," he said aloud.

"Ah," said a voice directly behind him, "but Forrest does. He also has legs."

Peter turned around, scared out of his skin, to see Ray the Taller smiling at him. Behind Ray the Taller was the rest of the company, sitting in a clump around a makeshift fire pit, on some soft mossy grass just a few yards in from the cliff edge.

"We're cooking. Something good, I hope. You shouldn't be on your journey without food."

Ray the Taller made a little gasping noise and looked intently at Peter's face.

"You've got a beard raising on your face, lad."

"How old do I look?"

Ray was taken aback with this question and didn't know quite how to put it.

"Son, you look at least thirty years old."

Well, that does it, thought Peter. He was aging fast and his time was short.

"Are you going to be able to help me?" asked Peter.

"I can point you in the right direction, but..."

Peter realized something for the first time since he met these people. Despite their hospitality and friendliness, they weren't on his journey, but their own, and with the ship supposedly grounded, they would have to wait for the tide and get back on their way.

"So, you are waiting for the tide to come in?"

"We don't need to wait for that."

"How are you going to get the ship back in the water?"

"He'll turn around when he wants."

"In my world," said Peter, "we refer to all of our ships as 'she' or 'her.'"

"Confusing," said Ray, "unless they tell you if it's all right. I know plenty of horse carts who prefer not to be referred to by any honorific or gender specific personal pronouns. I guess you just have to ask."

Peter nodded. "So, you're not going with me?"

"Oh no, Peter, we can't. It would put our families in danger. We can't do that. Besides," he continued, "Ray is so set on finding the portal to your world, it would destroy him to turn back."

Peter agreed. It was also the first time while in Innerworld that he didn't argue with his own mind about what was real and what wasn't. What Ray said made sense, and in all the fantasy stories Peter had read, the young boy or girl must be on his or her own at some point. *It had come to it,* he thought.

"Do you know how to get to the portal?" asked Peter.

"I'm assuming it is inland from Far Rock, in the Lasting Greenland's."

"About a day's journey, but it might not look like what you think. The last time I saw it, it looked like an open door in the middle of a field, quite far from where I thought I entered. If you find it and go through it, you should be in a chamber with a stone staircase winding upward. That will take you to another door that leads into the bottom of an old, dry water well. How you get out of that I'll never know."

Ray looked excited, and yet a little sad. "I know," he said, "this means good-bye, but we'll be all right you know; we have supplies and Durice and Novali have packed plenty for you, including extra clothes. You seem to be growing out of yours."

Peter agreed and added that he thought he was growing old rapidly, and didn't know if he could finish his task. He didn't even know what the magic vessels he was looking for actually looked like.

"Do you know which direction Covenswold is?" asked Ray the Taller.

"I don't have a clue."

"It is due east. We are facing, well, I'm facing south and you're facing north. So, if you go off to your right, you will eventually find the main road. It will be wild country for a while, but just stay on the path, and you'll be fine. If you see a giant schlurrg, don't panic."

"What am I supposed to do, play dead?"

"No, run like you've never run before because it will eat you, and rather sloppily."

Peter grimaced. "My head hurts," he said.

"Yeah," said Ray, "looks like that kukyz hit you hard. Don't worry, it managed to get washed over the side before we beached. I don't think it will be bothering us anymore."

"What hit me?"

"The little spy you saw on deck."

"Well, if I ever see it again, I hope to return the favor." He walked with Ray over to the fire pit, sat for a while and had something to eat, and Durice and Novali started to hum.

Ray the Shorter had a lute, or something like a lute, with him and was playing a soft, lulling tune.

Durice started to sing:
"In many lands and many isles
The ones I often dream of
There are many folks
And many things

That never ate a bean loaf...”
Peter chuckled.

Novali whispered, “It's an old sales song, when we had a bakery in Givenchy, just outside of Covenswold. We sold a lot of bean loafs.”

The two Rays joined in:

“Bean loafs, Bean loafs
Loafs that are made of beans
Buy some and eat one
Cause two will split the seams”

Ray the Shorter sang in a very low register:

“Of your trousers.”

Durice turned to Peter, “So we started up a tailoring shop as well.”

FOG AND SPECTACULAR NEWS

"So," began Bucky, with a little reluctance, "You're a ghost?"

"Ooh!" said The Beautiful Woman. "Scary!" She then proceeded to take the Afghan off the back of the muddy chair she was sitting on and drape it over her head. Feeling quite ghostlike she waved her arms around moaning, "boo," and then giggled. Pulling the Afghan off of her head she smiled broadly. "No, I don't think so."

Clement was getting upset, and a little scared; although, she was a very sweet ghost, if indeed she was one.

"Well, what are you then?" he almost yelled out, quite exasperated.

"I am The Beautiful Woman All Dressed in White."

"Oh, for crying out loud," yelled Clement, "what does that mean?"

"I'm pretty, and I'm dressed..."

"Like someone who got left at the side of the road on her prom," is what Bert said. "Sorry, dear, but it does look that way." He smiled, but it didn't seem to help.

"But the mud is..." and she got cut off again, this time by Mrs. Newcastle.

"All over the house. All over my powder blue wallpaper, all over the furniture, all over the children. Honestly, honey, dead or not you don't have to be so working class."

"See here," said Bert, who was very good at his job.

"Oh, sorry Bert, I meant, I really like you, blue collar and all..."

This made The Beautiful Woman smile broadly.

"See? We're all making friends!"

Mrs. Newcastle, who was holding the cord to the vacuum, let it drop and sat down in the soggy cushion of Bucky's chair.

"I'm tired. I'm tired of running, of riddles and of mud."

"Ah," said The Beautiful Woman, "I'll take care of the mud." She closed her eyes, scrunched up her nose and in a moment that no one there could define, there was no mud, no dirt, no puddles in the foyer, no smudges or smears anywhere, and all the crumbs from the cookies Bert had spit out were gone.

"That's what I'm on about," added Bucky, "How do you do that?"

"I know! Isn't it fun?" said the Beautiful Woman all Dressed in White again.

Bucky's mom, stood up again. She was impressed and surprised, but she needed answers and she wasn't going to play at guessing games, so The Beautiful Woman told her.

"I wore heels too big for me and I fell off the modeling runway during a fashion show here in Bright Lights."

"When?" asked Mrs. Newcastle.

"I don't know. You see, afterwards I forgot almost everything, and it took a long time I guess for me to remember what I do remember. You must understand, there is no 'time' where I'm now from. I could have died yesterday, or one hundred years from now. I really couldn't tell you."

"Well," said Mrs. Newcastle, "you're on the cover of last week's Fashion Faux Pas wearing red and orange."

"Don't really remember that. Would I have done that? Ooh! I guess that means I'm alive in this time. I better not run into myself. That would be funny. How do I tell me I'm the spirit of my dead self and having a lot of fun? Maybe I could sneak into the fashion show and watch what will happen to me. I'd love to see that!"

Clement, who was a little disturbed at all this talk about an afterlife decided he also wanted some answers.

"I just need to know what we're going to do about them," and he pointed to the window, where a dozen or more lizard rat monkey creatures called kukyz were leering in and watching them.

The Beautiful Woman stood up and smoothed out her pristine white gown, folded the Afghan and placed it on the back of the chair and stood there, with a commanding presence.

"We shall all go to the Chamber of Commerce," she said. "That's where he might strike his most drastic blow."

"OK," said Bert, "who and why?"

"Politikus Mediosus, and because he wants to take over both worlds. Your world and his are colliding on a regular basis. Most dimensions affect one another, like vibrations from a string after it is plucked, but these two are like twins. They are close together on the cosmic level of things and often interfere with one another. He was from this world, so it is said, and he wants it for his own, but he's not willing to give up the other, now that he has had it for so long."

Bert looked serious, and solemn. "Why the Chamber of Commerce?"

"He thinks that's where the economic seat of control is."

"It isn't."

"I know. He's an idiot. But he's powerful and power in the hands of an idiot can be terrifying, deadly, and sometimes...hilarious," she started to giggle and then caught herself, "but not now."

There was a sound like a pop and a crackle, and then the TV came on full blast.

"Sorry," said Clement, "I sat on the remote."

"That's all right," said Bucky's mom, "it's the news."

The two newscasters, all perfect in their well-made hair and serious looking faces, were dealing with a real problem.

"And so, Angela, it looks like this creeping fog is going to be around for a long time."

The TV showed pictures of a low-lying fog, falling over rocks and moving around cars and houses, obscuring traffic signals and peeping through keyholes into people's homes; people who happened to take video pictures with their smart phones and send the pictures to the news station.

"Oh my," said The Beautiful Woman. "The rain stopped, the agents are here and now the war really begins."

The newscaster named Angela spoke up next. "Ted, we seem to have some floating objects in the fog," and there was some silence.

"I'm Phil, Angela. Ted got... Ted moved on."

The TV now had pictures of uprooted trees floating almost motionless off the ground by several feet, and some mail boxes and baseball equipment. Clement was almost certain he saw a badger in a leisure suit.

"Yes, Angela, we have had a ton of rain, and now this low-lying fog covering the entire county, followed by scattered antigravity."

"So," followed up Angela, "if you are planning on going out tonight, please take a flashlight and lead boots."

Bucky's mom looked at Bucky, who then looked at Clement who was watching the Beautiful Woman. She in turn had her eyes glued on the set, and Bert was finishing up what cookies had been left on the table.

"So that's it for us here tonight. Remember, it's not news; it's SPECTACULAR!" and then Mrs. Newcastle turned off the TV.

"What does this mean?"

The Beautiful Woman went into the foyer and got everyone's coats and brought them back. She picked up the sprinkler key and handed it to Bert.

"It means there is a lot to do. Mediosus is flooding your world with his ability to deceive. Sure, there are floating objects, and there is a fog obscuring true vision, but it is nothing compared to what he has in store. He will strike hardest at the Chamber, so we must be off if we are to defend this world."

"Was that badger wearing a suit?" asked Clement.

"No dear," said Bucky's mom, "that would be too fantastic."

Bucky, after sitting patiently and taking all this in, finally spoke.

"And how are we to defeat him?"

"Oh, I don't know. It sure will be fun finding out! Let's go!"

With a turn she was out the front door, fighting off kukyz and laughing and spinning around. The others followed and soon between The Beautiful Woman and Bert, they managed to clear a path through all the kukyz. Several of them kept following behind and yelling out that they could get the best prices on medicine from Canada.

GIANT SCHLURRGS

The fire was warm and really not needed except for cooking, for the day was at its peak, and Peter smiled. He scratched his whiskers.

"I guess I should leave, if I'm going to live long enough to get wherever that place is I'm supposed to go."

Ray the Shorter made a hush noise, and then all was silent.

Peter whispered, "What?"

"We have a little friend," and Ray the Shorter pointed to the edge of the clearing near the makeshift camp.

Sitting on its haunches was the beast that Peter saw the night before on the deck of the Forrest, but this time it just looked pathetic. It was wet and scroungy. The thing had been tossed off the edge of the boat but managed to swim to shore and scramble up the pathway, following them. Probably it followed Peter, so he thought.

"Should we scare it away?" whispered Peter.

"Shh."

Then something remarkable happened. It walked up to the fire; although it was daylight and warm, it looked like it needed to dry off. It shook itself and got them all wet. It held out its claws toward the flame as if to warm them.

"So," it said, "you are our one-millionth visitor. Claim your prize."

Ray the Taller took a hot coal and threw it at the thing before it could scorch his own hand, and hit the kukyz square in the forehead.

"Really!" it said indignantly, and off it ran into the brush.

Peter stood up, kissed the two women, shook hands with the two Rays, shouldered the knapsack that Durice and Novai made for him and started off in the wrong direction.

"No, Peter," said Ray the Taller. "Turn around; you need to head east."

"How can you tell when you can't see the sun?"

Both Rays looked at each other. Durice and Novali frowned a bit. Finally, Novali spoke.

"We've always known. Everyone in Innerworld knows where everything is. We just do."

Ray the Shorter added, "We never thought someone from outside our world wouldn't know. But I guess it makes sense. How do you know which direction to go in your world?"

Peter looked down at his feet for a moment and thought.

"I always asked my grandma."

He turned toward what he now knew was east and started his long, lonely journey. After a while he could hear in the distance behind him a new song about lotions that cured a skin rash. Apparently, it occurred when eating too much bean loaf.

Within perhaps an hour the surroundings had grown increasingly full of trees, shrubs and lots and lots of green. Even in Innerworld moss grew on the north side of the trees. There was a brook flowing on his left, and it gave a soft mist, looking not unlike cotton on the top of the water in certain places. The path had long ago disappeared, and Peter wasn't sure if he was still heading in the right direction, except for the moss growing on the north side of the trees. So, if he kept that in his head, while it was still light out, he could find himself moving as much to the east as he could make out.

After what seemed like the whole morning, he came upon a clearing where there was a large, beautiful lake, all gray like glass, and still. Ahead of him near the eastern shore there were pines and oaks, and a full, green carpet of tall grass. Walking slowly to the lake's edge was a family of deer.

"Well, at least they have normal animals in Innerworld," Peter said to himself. He walked softly to the lake edge, still quite a distance from the deer. They didn't seem to care, and he felt good about that. He stopped, reached into the sack he had on his shoulder and found a leather bladder for water. He dipped it into the cool, clear and sparkling lake and filled it up, but not before taking a drink himself, for he was thirsty. It was the most delicious water he had tasted in what seemed a lifetime.

Looking into the water he saw what he thought were fish, but then the animals came up closer to the surface. They looked more like dogs, with large floppy ear-like appendages above their gills.

"Probably related to the seal," he thought.

Having another drink and filling his leather bottle, he again started east, and it was turning dusk.

He could hear his footsteps, crunching on the pine needles under his feet. He could also hear something else behind him and on his right. For the last hour the path had taken him east, but also northeast and away from the beach. Now with no path to follow, he was surrounded by deep green and the instinct to run was only stopped by the terrible knowledge that he didn't know where to run.

This of course, made him quite nervous, because he had no desire to run into a giant schlurrg. Had he thought about it, he would have realized he never ran into a giant schlurrg. Instead, it ran up behind him.

While the thing was still trying to be quiet, Peter sensed it was behind him, and he turned quickly, only to see one of the most horrific monsters he could ever have dreamed of, and wished he hadn't. Standing a good twenty feet taller, with scales that looked like deli meat slices and a mouth all wide and drooling, with very small, beady yellow eyes on either side of the upper jaw, and a third one on its forehead, was a giant schlurrg. It stood on two long, bumpy and boney legs. It had two short but dangerous looking arms with talons the size of baseball bats reaching for him. Its ugliness was only matched by the size of its razor-sharp fangs, sometimes hidden by its duel soaked lips; dozens of teath, all ready to scoop Peter up and crunch him in two.

So, Peter threw caution to the wind and took Ray's advice and ran as fast as he could. Over bracken, branches and brambles he ran. Stumbling and slipping, he ran as fast as he could. At first, he had gained some distance, but now the schlurrg was coming up fast, growling and gurgling, and no matter how fast Peter ran, it was as if this thing was always just an arm's reach behind him.

When Peter thought he could run no more, he turned to face his enemy and probably his end, when crashing through the trees on the south was a giant ship, on two legs and two arms, crawling fast toward the schlurrg. On the prow were Ray and Ray, shouting and yelling and whooping it up.

This caught the schlurrg by surprise. In all its life, it had never been chased by a sea faring vessel. So, it did what giant schlurrgs usually do when faced down by an enemy? It lay down and rolled on its back, obviously giving deference to Forrest, who, when sensing this, just stopped. Ray and Ray caught themselves before the sudden jar of the ship stopping would have thrown them into the trees.

Forrest reached over with his right hand and scratched the schlurrg on the belly, and turned around and trudged back toward the sea.

"You'll be all right, Peter!" yelled Ray the Shorter. Peter just stood there, watching a ship made of rock and trees, with arms and legs crawl back through the trees, knocking them over, and squashing ferns and such as it went. The schlurrg got up and followed, wagging its scaly tail behind it as it went.

Peter realized he had been holding his breath this whole time and finally let it out. After a few seconds of gathering his nerves, he turned back to his task, only to find the chase had taken him down and around and up the other side of the lake, and led him to a wide, paved road, going in what

Peter assumed was the right direction.

He started to walk and, after maybe ten steps, his legs gave out. What with all the running, the fear and the sheer exhaustion of growing up so fast, he simply couldn't take another step and passed out right there on the road.

SIZABLE QUANTUM VORTEXES

It was dark already and Bucky's group was marching as fast as they could, but the fog was really thick and low on the ground, making it hard to see where one was stepping. The Beautiful Woman had given them the power to walk in antigravity. Bert was out in front, brandishing his dangerous sprinkler key so none of the kukyz would even think of attacking. Most of them just stood off to the side or followed several yards behind them, whispering things like, "Your arrest record is now available," or more sinister things like, "Your account is about to be closed," and even though Bucky and Clement didn't know what all that meant, they could see in the eyes of the grown-ups that it wasn't very pleasant.

A Volkswagen slowly floated by. No one cared to notice. They were all intent on getting downtown and to building 301 A on E Street. That was where the business people had their chamber meetings. That was where the hideous war of Politikus Mediosus was thought to take place for the domination of the world. No, to be exact, the domination of two worlds. Then where would it end? If, as the Beautiful Woman suggested, there were multiple dimensions spanning eternity, then he could really cause some damage if he knew how to cross from one world to another. He could go almost anywhere. At least, that was what Bucky was thinking. She voiced her concern to Clement, who was walking closer and closer to the Beautiful Woman the more the fog thickened.

Bucky's concerns bothered him even more. He took the Beautiful Woman's hand in his.

"Don't fall in love," she said.

"What?" said Clement. "I'm just scared. I know you're too old. Don't be silly."

"I mean it's because I'm a spirit."

He grasped her hand tighter.

"You're hand feels real enough."

She giggled. "Oh yes. It's fun to have hands again. And toes! I love to dance on them." Then she just stood on her toes and did a few twirls. She clapped her hands and found delight in waving the fog around like smoke.

"Why do you act like a child?" asked Bucky.

"That's what we are. We're perpetually playful." Then she got serious again. "But we still have work to do. Oh look!" She pointed up in the air only a few feet. "There's a kind woman I wanted to meet."

"Good heavens!" exclaimed Bucky. "That's Mrs. Nesbitt, Peter's grandma!"

"I knew I wanted to meet her."

Indeed, there was Mrs. Nesbitt, floating a few feet above them, asking politely if someone could pull her back down to the sidewalk. Bert held his sprinkler key up so Mrs. Nesbitt could grab it and he was able to pull her down. It was unusual, but while the party was in the presence of the Beautiful Woman, they didn't at all feel the effects of the antigravity.

Mrs. Nesbitt calmed down a bit, because she had been really flustered by all the floating about, and a six-channel surround sound stereo system in a cabinet floated by them and almost hit her in the head.

"That would have been nasty," she said.

"And in surround sound, no less," added Clement.

The Beautiful Woman went on to say that the antigravity was designed to disable any defenses that might be surrounding the chamber.

"We have no defenses," said Bucky with some annoyance. "We're a small, sleepy town without any kind of important things an emperor or evil genius would want."

"But he doesn't know that, Bucky," said the Beautiful Woman. "He's cunning and resourceful, but he's still an idiot. Doesn't read. Can't for the life of me figure out how he duped a whole world in another dimension to be their great leader."

Grandma Nesbitt was obviously confused, scared and worried about Peter. She hadn't seen him for what was going on four days, so Bucky quickly told her all about their adventures and what Peter was trying to do.

"How can I help?" asked Grandma Nesbitt.

"When we get to where we're going, do whatever you think is best."

Then the Beautiful Woman was quiet for a while. Bucky asked her, after a few moments, if something was bothering her.

"Well, yes, Bucky. Quite frankly I'm wondering why all the kukyz have gone."

For the entire time they were calming Mrs. Nesbitt down and explaining the fantastic goings on, they hadn't noticed that the kukyz were no longer following them, or standing off to the side, or anywhere that could be seen.

"Maybe they went home," said Clement.

"Doubtful. I hope they're not planning a massive attack using SQVs."

"Now that," said Bert, "sounds like a weapon."

"And a nasty one at that," added the Beautiful Woman. "The one thing that could stop me, and mess up my hair if I'm not careful."

Bucky tried to figure out the initials but was having a hard time. "I don't even know what SUV stands for but I know it's a van. What's an SQV?"

"Sizable Quantum Vortex."

Bucky stopped suddenly and looked right at the Beautiful Woman All Dressed in White.   "That," she said, "is an oxymoron. If it's quantum it has no noticeable size."

"That's why they're particularly nasty." She kept walking and everyone followed.

Daybreak was still several hours away, and the night was cold. Bucky's feet hurt and Clement's shoulders ached. He also was having trouble breathing, what with the cold and the fog. Before the hour was up, however, they had made it to 301 A on E Street, and there was nothing to stop them from going into the building. There were no kukyz, no obstructions of any kind, and things that had been floating by, like flower pots and small animals, were all now on the ground again. Some of the pots were broken and the small animals had scurried home or decided to wander a bit and find something to eat.

"Do we just go up and knock?" asked Bert.

"No," said the Beautiful Woman. "I'm not sure how to protect it. Or what he is going to try to do. But I'm sure he thinks this is a chamber, like a room, and not an organization of any kind. He's in for a big disappointment. That will make matters worse. Idiots who are angry do very bad things to innocent people."

The wind picked up. There was some lightning, and a clap of thunder, but no rain. The fog rolled back, and in the sky above the building that was 301 A on E Street, the sky opened up like a hideous green fissure. The fissure closed again and then opened like a camera iris, and slowly the fog and clouds around it began to swirl. A loud rushing noise filled all their ears.

"Uhm," said the Beautiful Woman, "this is what I was afraid of."

As if on cue, thousands of kukyz spilled out of the hole in the sky. They landed on the street in clumps and more clumps. They weren't whispering anything anymore, but growling and baring their tiny fangs. With their claws extended they rushed upon the group, and pushing Clement and Bucky out of the way, they grabbed the Beautiful Woman All Dressed in White. With many snarls and clamping of their teeth, hideous little giggles and cackles, they dragged her up into the vortex in the sky, which promptly closed behind them. There was another clasp of thunder and then silence. Bucky and Clement, Grandma Nesbitt and Mrs. Newcastle, and Bert, were all alone except for each other.

Then the sky opened up again, and millions of kukyz rained onto the building until it was covered by them. Within a split second, they became still as stone. In fact, they had become stone, and the building known as 301 A on E Street, where the Chamber of Commerce met to have mixers and bingo night, was cocooned in solid rock.

"We've lost her!" cried Clement.

"We've lost," stated Bucky, with a quiet severity that sent a shiver down Clement's spine.

THE INFLUENCE OF POLITIKUS MEDIOSUS

Peter woke up in bed.

"Ah, I was right," he thought, "I'm in a hospital."

Yet, he really wasn't. He was in a firm, large and comfy bed, but there were no hospital walls or TV or trays or railings or anything else that you would find in a hospital. Instead, there were trees and small animals running about on the forest floor, and what felt like sunlight on his face, and a soft, balmy breeze blowing over him. He was outside, and in a bed that seemed to get snugger and comfier every time he tried to move. He didn't want to move much, because the comfort was luxurious.

In front of him and to his right was a large pane of glass in a frame, about the size of a man. Further to his right was a house on stilts. The stilts were apparently carved to look like chicken legs, but other than that, the house looked quite like a normal cabin in the woods. It was small, but still; it didn't look out of place except for the four chicken leg stilts. To his left was more forest, and finally, if he squinted and tried hard enough, he could see the road.

Directly in front of him, over the foot of the bed, he could see the deep forest. The fog was ghostly yet beautiful; mysterious yet inviting. There was morning dew on every green plant, every multicolored flower, and even his bed clothes. He did not mind, however, because it seemed natural, like a long-lost friend.

Peter finally got out of the bed, stood up and stretched. His arms ached and so did his back and legs. He never felt such pain before, and it startled him.

He could see better across the road south of him, and he saw another similar lake and it was very beautiful. It was, after all, the same lake from the other side. The water looked like silver. There were silver rivulets pouring into it from the mountain's further west. One mountain rose so high and was so majestic and colorful--red, brown, purple and capped with white--that Peter almost felt he was again back in his own world. Yet if he was, it was a different time, perhaps a younger world. At least that was how it felt. However, as he looked intently at the peak of the nearest, or perhaps largest, mountain, he could almost see the top of the eternally large cavern that made up Innerworld. It was hazy and difficult to see that far, but he almost could make it out. The most annoying thing was, however, that his eyes were getting blurry and they started to burn a bit. They watered and he wiped them dry with his sleeve.

Interestingly enough, his clothes seemed to fit better, or at least looser, than they did before.

"Maybe the process is reversing itself," thought Peter.

He looked around again, hoping to see someone that could help him understand where he was and what had happened to him. Through the pane of glass near his bed he could see the grassy yard beyond, and another bed outside, and an old man looking intently at him.

The old man had a gray and white beard and was very thin. His hair was long and straggly, and his face drawn and troubled. The old man just stared at Peter and didn't move.

Peter didn't know what to do or what to say, so he just walked slowly toward the old man. Apparently, the old man had felt or looked like he felt the same confusion and walked, at the same time it seemed, toward Peter.

When Peter got to the pane of glass he froze, and so did the old man. It wasn't a pane of clear window-like glass at all, but a mirror. The bed on the other side was the bed that Peter had been sleeping in, and the old man in the mirror was Peter himself.

This was so startling, Peter fell down in the grass, and that hurt his back even more.

All he could think of to say was, "Help." That word came out of his mouth so feeble that he felt really alone and helpless.

In a moment the door to the house opened and out stepped a very old woman. There was a wooden staircase or step ladder leading up to her door, and she slowly walked down it.

"I heard you call for help, my friend."

Peter thought all this looked too familiar and he remembered old fairy tales of a house on chicken-like legs in a deep forest, where an old witch would wait to catch people. He stood up as fast as his old bones would let him and held out his hand in warning.

"Don't come any closer, old witch. I know who and what you are."

"Not me, good sir. I didn't grow this house. I moved in three or four weeks ago, so you must have me mistaken for someone else. I wish to help you, for that is what I was told to do."

Peter walked back to the bed and sat down to give his back some relief. He thought hard, looking back in his memory over the last few days. *Not all ugly things are evil, and not all beautiful things are good,* he was told by the Beautiful Woman Dressed All in White.

"Are you evil, or are you good?"

"I should be asking you that question, mister."

"How did I get here?"

The old woman walked up closer.

"I found you on the road, and you were very tired, but I helped you up and you were able to make it this far. I'm sorry I don't have a room for you, but the forest is kind, and the beds here are well grown. You slept well? Are you hungry?"

Peter was very hungry and wanted to eat, but he didn't know what to think. Should he trust her or not?

"In my world," he started, "we have a legend of an old woman living in a house like that," and he pointed to the house on chicken leg stilts. "She is an evil witch."

"I don't know much, but I was exiled from Covenswold in South Folsborn because I studied such tales of other worlds. What I do know is this," and she began to explain something that Peter hadn't thought about. In other worlds, there are parallel experiences and phenomena. What happens in one, if it is close or linked to another, is mirrored in some way. It may be entirely different in nature, but may contain similar themes or ideas or names. He asked her for an example.

"Well, I don't know what your world is like, but I am aware of who you are, for the Beautiful Woman All Dressed in White has asked me to help you, so I will do my best to explain and ease your worry."

"Is she here?"

"No, I haven't seen her for four days. You asked for an example. Here is one."

She told of the Unknown Worlds Cluster, a group of alternate dimensions that often crossed one another in a sort of metaphysical dance. In one of the clusters, there were domesticated animals called stink rats. The stink rats would do tricks, play with the children, and even communicate on a rudimentary level with the human-like inhabitants. In another part of the cluster, the stink rats kept humans as pets, but the idea was the same.

"And the smell is as bad in one dimension as in another. Perhaps what is evil in your world, may be good in ours, or at least, neutral? Or the same, I don't really know."

"She did make me the best pancakes I have ever eaten." Peter was referring to the Beautiful Woman all Dressed in White.

"Ah! A dish from your world?"

"Yes, exactly the same."

"She should know; she was originally from your world. So was that evil wizard of a tyrant, Politikus Mediosus."

"I've been growing old, very old since I've been here, only four days, and she looks timeless."

"She is not what you are anymore, and Politikus has had some dealings with the Evil One, which gave him power over age. This is his great advantage; although he is dim in thought, he is at least street wise, and can persuade others easily enough through many years of practicing deceit, and not growing old."

The house lifted a chicken leg and with it rubbed its door under the door latch.

"Did that house just scratch its nose?"

"Oh, probably. It has a cold. It's terrible when I'm in it. Everything breaks and I have to go back into Givenchy and buy everything all over again. Waste of money, this house."

Peter's head was getting dizzy and he needed something to eat. He looked around for his knapsack. It wasn't there.

"Where are my things?"

The old woman laughed a hacking laugh and apologized for putting it in the house. She hobbled back to the house and went in. Peter just sat there, wanting very much to go to sleep.

In a moment or two she returned with his sack and handed it to him. He thanked her and looked around in it for some food. He took out what was possibly a bean loaf and started eating. It wasn't too remarkable, but it did the trick. The old woman looked on with serious hunger in her eyes. It wasn't a scary look, but one that made Peter feel pity.

"Why, madam! You're starving," he said.

"It is true, I haven't eaten in days. After I was exiled, I found this place. I don't even know if the owner will return and if he or she does, what will be done to me."

"You need this more than me," and he gave her the largest portion of his food. He also dug around in his pack and found that Ray and Ray had left him with a purse. He took it out, and in it was a substantial amount of gold coins.

"I don't know how much these are worth, but you can have them. You can have them all."

She looked genuinely surprised. "How? How can you do this?"

Peter thought for a moment and made up his mind that he was to forge on ahead with his quest, imaginary or not.

"I don't need money or food where I'm going. I will more than likely die of old age before I get there, and that is not far off if I'm aging as fast as I think. The only thing is, I wish I could do what I have to do. I'm a failure, I think." He started to cry a bit.

She sat down next to him and put her arms around his shoulder. She smelled sweet, like flowers and springtime.

"What exactly is it you have to do to face Politikus?"

"What all did she tell you?" asked Peter, who was drying his eyes on his loosely fitting sleeve.

"Only that you're the one, the prophesied one who will come and deliver us from this tyrant."

"What has he done that is so awful?"

"He has corrupted the minds of the people. Those of us who still think for ourselves are exiled or killed. He wishes to do the same in your world, and others if he can. He is drunk or mad with power. He loves lies. Somehow, if he can deceive others, he gets stronger-more powerful."

Peter decided to trust her, and after apologizing for being rude and not introducing himself, they exchanged names and other pleasantries.

"I'm Peter," he said.

"And my name is Iggy. Although I don't think I look like it."

Peter wasn't sure what she meant, or what to say next, but Iggy ate the food Peter gave her and she felt better.

"You are very generous, Peter. For in pouring out your purse, you have poured out your heart, and trusted one that you felt might be a danger. You will go far, and you will accomplish this task that has been given you, here and in your own home."

"Thank you for your encouragement, Iggy, but I have no strength left."

"That is the last of it, I guess," said Iggy, "but you are so close. Givenchy is very close to Covenswold. You are almost there. There is a young wizard who lives there, and he may know of these magic vessels. Be very careful what you tell him, however; I don't know that much about him. It may be best to avoid him. Follow your own instincts in this matter. Listen to the wisdom of She who is in White, because she is innocent. These people in Covenswold are or have been easily swayed to teachings I find disquieting. Something may sound like the truth, or very close to it, but is a dangerous lie. Unfortunately, most of those people think they are believing the truth. They are powerless against Mediosus's guile."

Peter thanked her and kissed her on her cheek. She blushed just a tiny bit. He got up and asked which way to Covenswold and she directed him.

"If I'm to find these three vessels, I'll have to ask someone."

"Better to avoid anyone who has authority or respect in that hated city. Remember, it may sound like truth, but it is a lie."

Peter nodded, and started what looked like a long and weary walk into an unknown and dark danger.

THE BATTLE OF MARSDON HILL

Grandma Nesbitt stomped her foot.

"Well, I haven't lost," she said vehemently, "neither has Peter if I know him. Whatever is going on here, we must do something. We must take a stand."

The rest agreed but without the Beautiful Woman All Dressed in White to guide them, they didn't know where to begin.

"We can't get into the building; they've blocked it up. What a disappointment it will be for them to find out it only has day old cupcakes and cold coffee in the rec room," said Bert.

Clement looked at Bucky and offered up an idea.

"We could find a way in, you know, underground and such. Maybe if we go into the sewer, we can come up through the air vents and protect what is in there."

Bucky didn't mean to be rude but she shot down that idea quick. "There is nothing in there. The Chamber of Commerce is not a 'chamber' at all. It is a group of people who--"

She was cut off rather tersely. Mrs. Nesbitt had found her own sprinkler key at the flower shop across the street. The flower pots had all fallen when the antigravity phenomenon had stopped, so there were broken shards of pots and spilled dirt everywhere, and the proprietor didn't notice her taking it.

"I'll return this when I'm done," she said as she tossed a twenty-dollar bill onto the upturned table in front of the shop, directly across the street from where the kukyz had covered 301 A.

"Now I'm going to do something or I'm in for it!" So, she stomped off toward Ewart Street School.

"Where are you going?" asked Bucky's mom.

"To the well where my grandson is! This place was a distraction. The real battle will happen at one of those portals, or my name isn't Nora Nesbitt!"

They all followed, determined to do something, anything, to thwart a hostile takeover, even if it was a magical one that they didn't understand.

"If it is a doorway in, then it is a doorway out," said Bucky.

This made sense to everybody and they all agreed to go. Next to the building known as 301 A, there was another shop, a thrift store of sorts, and there were a few TV sets in the street window that had somehow managed to not tip or fall during the antigravity effect and were currently on.

Grandma Nesbitt wanted to go have a look and see if they could figure out what they were up against. The group walked up to the thrift shop and stood, staring at the largest TV screen, where the Spectacular News was playing loud and clear.

"And so, Angela, there was another strange robbery in Hollywood again. Seems some big fan of special effects stole a whole lot of gelatin used in making artificial lava, and also a certain amount of floor heaters and smoke machines. They promptly sold it on that popular auction site, I-Lagoon, and the lucky auction winner is now wanted by the police. But here's something interesting about all those strange critters we've been seeing, it seems these cute little guys have been covering up buildings all along the East Coast as well. Strangely enough, they seem to mostly be churches, synagogues, temples, meeting halls, that kind of thing. They have been avoiding, however, fast food restaurants and banks."

"Well, they certainly are cute, Ted."

"Phil."

"I've decided from now on to call you Ted."

"Alrighty then."

"Cute," yelled Bucky, "they're simply hideous!"

Phil on the TV continued on, "Angela, some folks have been calling in saying these little guys are terrifying, so we've asked a scientific expert to come on our show and give us the low down on these entertaining and informative creatures."

The camera panned to the right of Phil to show a small man with very little hair on the top of his head, but a lot on his chin and upper lip. He also had tiny rimmed glasses that shone too much in the studio light.

"What we have here," said the little man, "is an entirely new species of either primate, reptile or rodent. Certainly, an unlikely evolution of all three."

"So, a new species? It just appeared?" asked Phil.

"No, Phil," said the little scientist, but he was interrupted.

"Ted," said Phil.

"I thought your name was Phil."

"It is, but Angela wants to call me Ted and..."

"Anyway," continued the scientist, "nothing is ever 'new.' I guess I could call it, 'newly discovered.' These creatures have probably been here for a long time."

"Since the stone age?" Phil asked, trying to look bright. "I mean, since they can turn to stone. You know? What other animal has evolution provided us that can turn to stone?"

"We don't know yet. That's the beauty of science. Some of us can make it up as we go."

The TV turned immediately to a commercial and Bucky got very frustrated.

"Science on news programs is no science at all. Who is that idiot anyway?"

"Phil," said Clement. Bucky meant the scientist, who really had no training in serious science at all but wrote a lot about how color can change the future and a series of science fiction stories that started a whole religion. He also denied the existence of China, citing he had never been there, and even though he had seen pictures and had reliable witnesses to tell him otherwise, he was going to refuse to believe it until he actually got there.

Bucky started walking faster. "I don't know about how the rest of you feel, but if our TV shows are trusting the words of lower intelligent life like that guy, we're already in the war."

The rest agreed and picked up their pace.

Within a few minutes they were on the grounds of Ewart Street School and marching straight toward the squeaky metal gate. Clement looked a bit worried, because this was where it all began, and it made him uncomfortable.

"I'm such a dolt. Why did I do it? Do you think Peter could ever forgive me?"

"No time to worry about that now, Clement. We have bigger problems."

Bucky was right. Above Marsdon Hill, where the well was, loomed a dark and ominous mist. In it were several flashing lights, like lightning balls or arcs of electricity. Every now and then a bolt would strike the well. The bolts increased in frequency as Bucky and the others made their way up the hill.

"I don't like the look of that," said Bert.

"Careful Bev, you're going too fast,' said her mother, but Bucky didn't listen. She climbed the hill and stood at the edge of the well, looking up into the dark cloud formation. Clement had run right up behind her.

"What can you see?"

"Nothing. It is too dark."

A lightning bolt flashed and hit the ground near the well. There was a loud clapping sound and the children fell back, their skin tingling with electricity.

"It's too dangerous!" yelled Grandma Nesbitt.

Suddenly from out of the well they heard a cry.

"Grandma?" said the voice from the well.

"Peter!" yelled Grandma Nesbitt and she ran as fast as her plump body could move and got to the well despite all the lightning.

"Are you all right down there?"

"I'm old."

Clement looked at Bucky. "Did he say he's cold?"

A loud horn sounded, coming from the clouds. Mrs. Nesbitt, who was a religious woman, thought this indeed was the final apocalypse. She looked up and started to sing a hymn when out of the sky and through the little roof and into the well drove a small ford convertible, the driver and passenger laughing and yelling, "Hello, Mom!" then disappearing into the gloom.

POTTY HARRISON AND THE CHAMBER OF COM-MERCE

Peter had enough of the bean loaf left to give him some energy, and he found himself walking with a little bit of spirit. He passed through Givenchy with very little to do but stop and rest. No one talked to him. They seemed preoccupied with not wanting to be noticed. Further on he found he was nearing what should have been a sea port city. It was small at first, but the further in he got the more buildings he could see. This was the remarkable thing because they were all round or oval in shape. The windows were open, without glass or shutters, and the buildings themselves looked as if they had roots. There was a large gate to the city, growing right out of the ground as if it were two trees joined in an arch high overhead. There were many people milling about, walking toward the inland ways of the city. There were none, however, near the beach. In fact, there were no ports, piers, or anchorages anywhere along the coast. It was as if the folks of Covenswold didn't care to have boats or even take a swim. The beach looked like it had never been walked on, the sand was so smooth.

Peter could hardly take a step when he entered through the broad gates to the city. There were strange writings across the arch of the gate that reminded him of the doorway in the well, what seemed like a lifetime ago.

No one seemed to notice him. He called out to a few people ahead of him on the road, walking in the same direction he was going, but they wouldn't turn around. As he tried to walk faster, he could feel his joints hurting so, and his back bending in an awkward position, as if he were perpetually leaning forward. Eventually he got up to someone and tapped the man on the back of his shoulder. The person didn't turn around but asked, "Who goes there?"

Peter caught up and passed the stranger and turned around to look at him. The man stopped short, rather shocked that someone would look him in the face.

"Sorry, but I'm getting on in years and you wouldn't turn around to see me. My name is Peter, and I'm looking for Covenswold."

"You're here, Peter. This is Covenswold. Where are you from?"

Peter looked down, trying to figure out how to explain it. "I'm from another land, across the sea." He waved in the direction of the ocean behind the man.

"What sea?"

"Why," said Peter, "the sea. There," and he pointed, "behind you."

The man looked at him as if he were crazy and started to laugh.

"You're an idiot, stranger. There is no sea behind me."

"Yes, there is, plain as day. Turn and look."

The man refused and kept walking. "There is nothing behind me."

Peter found he still had a little energy to run (even though it hurt) so he ran up to another stranger, a woman this time, and found he had to get in front of her as well just to talk to her.

"Where is everyone going?"

"Why, to get the truth of the day. What are you? A stranger?"

"Yes," said Peter, "from across the sea."

"What sea?"

"Not you, too!" and he took her by the shoulders and tried to turn her around so she could see the great ocean of water behind her, but she wouldn't budge.

"See here, old man, you're hurting me."

"I'm sorry, it's just that it is behind you, plain as day. You couldn't miss it."

"There is no sea, or ocean or anything behind me. There is nothing. This," and she pointed to what was ahead of her, the people, the street, the buildings, "is all there is. Nothing more. Now out of my way so I may get to the Fortress of Situational Ethics for the new truth."

Peter reluctantly moved to the side and she continued around him. He looked to where she was going and all he could see was a large myriad of people moving toward a very dark mountainous region, just outside the eastern side of the city. He couldn't tell, but it looked like there was a large blanket or sheet, or something of a material nature in the sky over that part of the city stretching out toward the dark region. It was too dark to make out what was there, but Peter guessed it was probably the fortress where Politikus Mediosus dwelt.

"If Mediosus says there is no sea, then there is no sea," said a young man, who was standing in the doorway of a small hovel, watching the crowd and most of all Peter.

"You believe that?"

"It doesn't matter what I believe. It is what he says, and the people trust him. He tells them what they need to know, true or not, and they follow."

Peter asked the young man who he was and the young man told Peter he was a magician, well skilled in the arts and quite capable of helping anyone in need of knowledge.

"How did you know I had such a need?"

"I wouldn't be a good magician if I didn't. Come in," and he disappeared into his hovel. Peter followed and noticed there was writing above the door. He couldn't read it.

"Is that your name?"

"What?"

"Above your door, there. I can't read your writing."

"Those are words I live by," said the magician, "they are, 'Do as Thou Wilt.'"

Peter sat down on a small wooden stool near the wall and leaned against it to take the ache out of his back. It didn't help.

"What's that supposed to mean?"

"The greatest service you can do humanity is to serve your own interests."

"Then I shouldn't have given Iggy all my money and most of my food."

The magician laughed. "You're an old fool. Here in Covenswold you will learn the truth. For however many days you have left. No one, simply no one helps others without some kind of payment or agenda. Since you have no money, I cannot help you."

"I thought so." Peter got up to leave.

"However," said the magician, stopping Peter at the door, "perhaps we could trade favors."

"What could I possibly do?"

The magician was suddenly very animated and excited.

"Do you have any influence over people? Especially people in high places? Tell me what you need and if I help you, you can help me advance."

"I don't know anyone here. I'm here to see Politikus and that's it."

"Well, that is someone of influence. Tell me what you need, and if you put in a good word for me, Ulster Crow, that's my name, then you will receive power and fame."

Peter remembered what Iggy warned him about. He was certain that this was not a man to be trusted. The man was young, and fit and full of life, certainly a youthful adventurous soul, but not all things beautiful are good. Not all things said are to be believed. The older he was getting, the easier it was for him to discern between what was fraud and what was real.

Peter started laughing.

"What," said Ulster, "is funny?"

"You're a liar and I know that. I find it much easier to figure that out, and yet, all this," and Peter waved his hands about, "this Innerworld, is part of my fertile imagination. And I'm dying, Ulster. I'm lying either at the bottom of a well, or in a hospital bed, dying. My body is failing me. The curse of being a child with a high IQ is that I can figure out these things at a young age." Peter never wanted to admit that Ewart Street School was for the gifted; he tried to play it down, but it was. He certainly had a brain for it and at this point it seemed to him to be a curse.

"So," Peter said, "I'm looking for three magic vessels that I must empty at an appropriate time, and in doing so, I will save this world, and my own."

"You really believe that?" asked Ulster, mocking Peter's old voice.

"For what it's worth," added Peter, "I do. For if this is all a hallucination, then by saving this world I will wake up. If it is real, I can die fulfilling a destiny I had no idea was mine."

Ulster didn't look too friendly anymore. "What makes you think we need saving?"

"You can't even admit you have an ocean behind you because some person, a person mind you, nothing more, tells you it isn't there. There is nothing wrong with believing in what you cannot see, but not believing in what is plainly before you and you refuse to see is folly."

Peter turned and left the hovel, but Ulster was not far behind.

"I respect your opinion, old man, but I think you are quite wrong. I don't need saving. I've saved myself."

"You can't even see an ocean behind you because you're too self-absorbed in serving your own interests. You can't see the danger that poses. Tides rise, and floods occur in this world and in mine. You and everyone else here have turned their backs on the truth. Who is quite wrong? You listen to a politician who controls all forms of communication in your world. In our world that's called spin, or propaganda. We have a similar problem. Very few people think for themselves. I've made up my mind. I can't see the gardener, but I know his handiwork, and I choose to acknowledge his skill and artistry."

Ulster looked confused. He obviously had missed something and said so.

"Doesn't matter, Ulster. I need to find these objects. Where is the marketplace?"

Ulster thought he wouldn't tell him, but he changed his mind. "You won't like it. You have to get on the net and shop there.

"The net? Did you say the net?"

"Yes, go to the Chamber of Commerce, which is a room at the center of town, and get onto the net. There you can do anything you like, be anyone you want, say anything to anyone. No one will recognize you. There are forbidden things you can do there. The only thing is, be aware that the kukyz will follow you everywhere you go on the net. That is where I learned my craft. That is where I spend most of my life. That is where Politikus is most powerful. You might meet him there.”

Then Ulster laughed an insidious laugh and went backwards into his home, so as not to turn around and see the ocean.

Peter continued to walk into town, wishing he had a walking stick, when he saw a group of people going into a round, cylindrical shaped building. It also looked like it was growing from the ground, though it had a steel color. Peter went in and all was dark.

As his eyes adjusted, he noticed a series of rope ladders that lead up to a large, net-like web of ropes that spanned the immense ceiling above him. Obviously, the cylinder-like building was only a means to get there, but the net covered the whole top of the city, connecting it to the dark of the mountains that surrounded Covenswold and narrowed toward the Fortress of Situational Ethics.

It took a mighty long time but Peter finally made it onto the net, and there were thousands upon thousands of kukyz, following thousands and thousands of people who had managed to walk the net like a street. Peter had to move on his hands and knees, grabbing the ropes of the net so as not to fall through it. Soon he was able to get used to it, almost by nature, and could stand.

He must have walked several miles, but he never saw a place of commerce that carried what he wanted. There were places where one could buy books or food or clothing. There were hidden places where it seemed crimes were being committed. People would sneak in and sneak out. Some would go in and stay and never come out until they were too hungry or too thirsty. Those certain people looked very sick in body, but there was still an enchantment over them. He couldn’t make out any distinctions on their faces. They were for all practical purposes, anonymous.

He did stop someone, however, who also looked like a blank face, and asked if that person knew where he could buy magic vessels, or how to get to the fortress of Politikus.

“Politikus will talk to anyone on the net. But you must be on the net. As for the vessels you seek, there is one magician besides the great Logician Mediosus, but he is back in town. Off the net for now. He comes here often though.”

“You mean Ulster?”

“Yes.”

“I have spoken to him. He doesn’t have what I want.” Peter kept walking in the direction of the dark mountains.

Hours passed. He walked slowly, both because he needed to keep his footing, but because he also was tired and he hurt so. The walls of rock around him and above him were indications he was now in the mountains, but it was dark and cold. He couldn't see well, and all the noise of the net was fading to a muffling sound.

He went through several tunnels where he had to get on his hands and knees and crawl. By the last tunnel, maybe the fifth he had crawled through, all light had gone and he couldn't see a thing.

He crawled like this for what seemed to be several hours. It could have been days, for all he knew. He was tired and thirsty and ever so weak. At one point he just lay down on the net and slept.

When he awoke, he thought he had gone blind. It was so dark and now there were no sounds at all. Perhaps he had died. Maybe this was death. Or, business hours were over and many of the people had gone home. One thing was for sure, the net was still there, for his hands were gripping tightly to it. So, he decided to keep moving in the direction he was headed.

More time slipped by; then there was a glimmer of light. After a few more yards of crawling, the light was dazzling and blinded him for a moment. When his eyes adjusted, he could see that he was over what looked like a river of fire or lava. The cave walls around him were glowing red with the hot light from the fire river, and Peter began to sweat profusely.

The walls were intricately carved with bas-reliefs of ancient animals, people and cities. This was obviously an interior chamber to some building. Perhaps it was the fortress of Politikus Mediosus himself. If so, Peter was a failure again, for he did not have the three magic vessels.

It all seemed so hopeless, but at least there was a ledge to his left, and he could walk on solid rock and not this net anymore. He moved slowly over to the ledge and stood on it. His feet hurt, and his back ached, and he was sweating profusely. His vision was blurred but he could see enough to keep from the edge. It would certainly be a fatal fall.

He put out his left hand to feel the wall and slowly continued forward when he noticed the net was tied off and there was nothing to keep him from falling into the lava anymore should he slip. Ahead of him and behind there were several kukyz moving about, nimbly jumping around him and grasping the ledge without the slightest worry of tumbling into the flames.

Peter sat down to rest. He stayed close to the wall, pulling his legs up by the knees, no matter how much it hurt, just to keep his feet from dangling over the edge. He heard a laugh coming from ahead of him.

I guess my hearing is all right, he thought. The laugh filled the chamber. In a flash there appeared on the ledge several yards ahead of him, a large and mighty man in a striking suit of armor.

The armor was glowing green, almost translucent, with a predominance of a darker green on the head and arms. His whole body was covered and yet he could move with agility. There was a mask like from the armor of old legends to cover his handsome face. The armored man carried a sword that had the same eldritch glow. He laughed again.

Peter got up, saw what a terrible match this would be, and decided perhaps he should go back and try harder to find the three magic vessels, despite his aging body. He turned to head back but standing behind him was Ulster, holding a very ugly yet clingy kukyz.

"You still want me to put in a good word for you?" asked Peter with some dripping sarcasm.

"That won't be necessary," said Ulster. The kukyz hissed at Peter.

"You didn't have to comment on my comment. It is obvious you two are working together.

"You're a smart old man," said Ulster, "but you should have listened to the old woman. I'm an enchanter, and I've been helping Mediocre here," and he was interrupted.

"Mediosus," the man in armor corrected him.

"Mediosus, with all my cunning. I could see you from afar, in my mind. I brought you here."

"No, no Ulster, that was me," said Mediosus, who indeed was the man in the armor, "I did that one."

"Details, details. Next, you'll be taking credit for moving the portal entrance to the Fortress of Situational Ethics."

"No, no. You did that. You did that well. A little dirty, but you can clean it up after all of," he waved his hands in a random manner, "this."

"You led me here," said Peter, wiping sweat from his brow with his loose-fitting sleeve, "so let's get this over with. What do you want from me?"

"Peter," said Mediosus, "if you really are the one who is to defeat me, don't you think I at least could have a chance to plead my case?"

"You've already won, Mediosus. I don't have the magic vessels and I'm too old and weak to fight you physically. So have done with it. I'm tired."

Mediosus just laughed. Ulster did too, but the look on his face seemed to indicate he didn't get the joke, whatever it was

"Come here, Peter, there is something I want you to see."

"Can't you come here and show me? I'm tired."

"No, no I cannot. You must come here, because what I have here behind this door," and he pointed to a part of the wall that Peter couldn't see clearly, "is so beautiful, so sweet, so innocent, that you'd have to see it to believe it."

"Oh, all right." Peter got up and slowly walked toward Politikus Mediosus, until the tyrant held out his hand and motioned for Peter to stop.

"Don't take another step, Peter. That part of the ledge is rigged to open up."

"Why?"

There was a familiar sound from the wall. Peter could just see a square window in the wall, obviously an opening into some prison. Inside was the Beautiful Woman All Dressed in White, chained to a slab of rock standing upright.

"If you want to know, she is slowly being let into the fire river below."

"I didn't want to know that," said Peter.

"Peter," said the Beautiful Woman, "whatever he says to you don't listen. I'm in no danger whatsoever."

Mediosus laughed again. Ulster laughed as well, and the little kukyz monster hissed.

"If you step on this part of the ledge," said Mediosus, "it will open downward, closing off the trap that she is slowly sliding through," and Peter could see she was slipping down, the rock and all, but slowly, as if she were sand in an hour glass.

"Yay! This is like a slide!" she said with a laugh.

"By stepping on this part of the ledge you will save her, but you will then be pitched into the river of fire yourself. So, you see, there is a choice here for you. You can fight me, but I'll kill you easily and she will die. Or, you can save her, and then you yourself will die in torment. I will live. Either way, Peter, you lose and I get what I want, your world."

"How?"

"Look above you."

Peter did and what he saw was a long and high tunnel, familiar looking, and outside of it, for there was an opening at the top, he saw a tiny roof and around that a swirling mass of clouds and a lightning storm of great power.

"That is your world. I've been invading it since you've been here. In a moment, the two of you will be dead, or at least one of you, and I will then take the Chamber of Commerce!"

"Not to rain on your parade," said Peter, with some disdain, "but the chamber of commerce is an organization of business people. Not an actual chamber."

Mediosus looked stunned.

"But my spies..."

"You've trained them well, to lie. They've even lied to you."

Mediosus waved his hand as if swatting at a fly. "It doesn't matter. I'll control the media, the political elite, the fast-food restaurants and possibly the public transit. That's a start."

The Beautiful Woman All Dressed in White was slowly slipping out of Peter's sight, but she was laughing.

"What's so funny?" asked Mediosus.

"You can't do anything to me. I've already died."

Several things happened at once. Peter didn't hear what the Beautiful Woman had said and he had made up his mind to save her anyway, so he stepped on the trap. Immediately it opened and he fell. At the same time several lightning blasts from above had struck the opening to the tunnel that led straight up. Ulster was shocked at Peter's stunning decision and tumbled in after him, screaming as he fell.

The fall wasn't long, for before Peter knew it, he had landed in the lava, but it wasn't lava at all. It was a gelatinous substance that reflected light from beneath. It wasn't hot; that heat came from furnaces down under the ledge. Peter wasn't really hurt at all, mostly. The river of fire wasn't deep. It was soft and shallow and not very far below the ledge he had been on. The only thing that was hurt was his already aching back, and he sat up.

"What is this," he cried out, "a joke?" Ulster wasn't laughing; he had landed on his head and had a nasty bump. The kukyz creature was also a bit shaken up. Mediosus was shocked.

"I didn't think you'd do it." He walked down a stone spiral staircase that was behind him and walked right up to Peter. Just then a door on the opposite wall opened and the Beautiful Woman all Dressed in White walked out, none the worse for wear and not chained to anything.

"That could have been more fun. Do you have a better slide?" and she started kicking the gelatin around and giggled.

"It's gelatin, Mediosus; your lava is a stage trick," said Peter.

"Why I'll be. Ulster?" Ulster hid his head in his hands. "I told you I wanted a flaming river of fire and smoke!"

"And that's what I got you. I went into Peter's world and found it all on the net. Which is a different kind of net there than what we have here. I paid good money for it off of an auction site. Probably shouldn't have trusted the dealer. Had only three feedback marks."

Peter laughed out loud. He couldn't believe the simplicity of evil. How the deceivers can be so easily deceived. Truth, he thought, is not like this. It is mature, simple in a different way, as in not complicated, and innocent. The Beautiful Woman approached Peter.

"You did it."

"He most certainly did not!" Mediosus was indignant. "He didn't find the three magic vessels and he didn't empty them at the appropriate time. I win! I win I tell you!"

"He's right," said Peter. "I've failed. I didn't know what to look for, or anything. I'm too old now, too feeble to be able to do anything."

"But you did do it, Peter. You emptied your mind while renewing it and filling it with more holy thoughts then you probably knew. You emptied your heart when you emptied your purse to help poor Iggy, whose life is forever changed by your kindness. And just now you emptied yourself of your life, to save someone else. Although it turned out to be a trick. Your heart was in the right place. And although I didn't need saving, since I already am, I still love you for it, Peter. You are a heroic person."

Peter looked stunned, and he was not sure how to respond.

"I'm not sure how to respond to all this."

Mediosus started up the stairs. "I'll tell you how I am going to respond. I'm going up that well and finish the war I started."

Ulster just moaned. He was covered in red and yellow gelatin.

Peter slowly got up. "I have to stop him," he said.

"Trust me, your act of selflessness will stop him in a way you can hardly imagine."

Peter nodded but still went slowly after Politikus Mediosus. All the while he was hobbling up the stairs, he was pulling pieces of gelatin off of his shirt. At the top of the winding staircase was the entrance to the Marsdon Hill well. Peter now could plainly see, there were notches for hands and feet cut into the well. Mediosus was several feet above him but Peter started to slowly climb after him. The firestorm of lightning and cloud and smoke outside of the well was intense. This was indeed, the same well Peter had fallen into.

"How did the well get here? And how did it grow hand and foot holds?" The Beautiful Woman had gone, but Politikus heard him, and mocked him with an answer.

"Because I have the know-how, and that's why! I did it! I invaded your world with confusion and the ceasing of all-natural law, and I moved this well to my palace and I..."

Peter heard something over Mediosus's self-glorifying monologue and tried to listen.

"It's too dangerous," he heard. That sounded like Grandma Nesbitt.

"Grandma?" Peter yelled. He wasn't sure, but he thought he heard her ask if he was all right.

"Well, I'm old, now." He wasn't sure she heard him because at the next moment there was the sound of a blaring car horn and plummeting down out of the sky in a burst of green smoke was his mother and father's Ford convertible. It was falling right toward the well entrance.

There were crashing sounds and the rushing of wind and more horn noises and the car fell right into the well, as if it were small enough to fit. The noise and sight were so distracting that Politikus did not get out of the way, but with a scream he was hit head on by the Harrisons and carried deep into the Innerworld well and beyond. As they passed Peter, who hugged the wall tenaciously, he heard his parents yell, "Good job, son. You look good for your age." Then they laughed and were out of sight. He could still hear Politikus yelling for them to stop but he couldn't see them anymore.

Without looking up, he reached to grab the next handhold, because he thought for sure he would fall, he felt so weak.

What surprised him was that he didn't grab a handhold at all, but a firm, feminine hand, that gave a strong pull and before he knew it, he was out of the well and sitting on its edge, Bucky Newcastle holding his hand and Clement patting him on the back. Mrs. Nesbitt was crying for joy and Mrs. Newcastle was hugging a man he didn't know. Yet it was all real, all home, all Marsdon Hill outside of Ewart Street School, all as real as it could be.

Peter was a boy again. Twelve years old and in his old man peasant clothes that Durice and Novali had given him. He breathed in the clean after storm air and looked at his friends and his grandmother.

"Was that my mom and dad?"

Grandma Nesbitt nodded.

"They're alive, then? Driving from dimension to dimension?"

She nodded again, tears flowing from her eyes.

Peter wanted to go home and he said so. He was tired and confused, and needed a little help in getting down Marsdon Hill, but with Bucky and Clement helping him, that got him back to Grandma Nesbitt's house where he slept the rest of the night and the whole next day.

EPILOGUE

Ten years later, Peter and Bev and Clement had an opportunity to take some college courses in Hawaii, so they flew out to California where they would take a cruise ship to the island.

They arrived at a port near San Diego and a huge, beautiful cruise ship awaited them, but Peter wanted some time alone. Bev and Clement had gone on ahead to the boat, while Peter walked along the beach. He could remember very little about what had happened, but what he did remember was that it happened, because Bev and Clement had their own adventures as well, and no one outside of Bright Lights ever knew, but he knew, and they knew, and so did Mrs. Newcastle, who was now Mrs. Flanagan, Bert's wife.

As Peter walked out a bit to the water, he saw someone running on the beach, then sitting down to watch the waves. She was a woman of unusual beauty, in a very blue sweatshirt and sweatpants, for the afternoon air was cool. Peter was not mistaken; it was her all right. It had to be. He ran up to her and startled her. He took her hand and she pulled it away.

"Don't you recognize me?"

"I'm sorry, mister, I don't."

"It's me. It's Peter Harrison, and you're the Beautiful Woman All dressed in White. Only now.. you're in sweats."

She frowned. A man approached her from up the beach. She got up and ran to him and said something. Peter walked slowly up to them. The man was dressed like the woman only in red.

"I'm sorry," said Peter, "you looked so familiar. I didn't mean to scare you."

"She gets that a lot," said the man. "She's a famous model, after all."

Bucky had told Peter all about their adventures in Bright Lights with the Beautiful Woman and the floating things and the rain and the kukyz and the fact that the Beautiful Woman had died at some time. It must be, thought

Peter, sometime yet to come. For in Heaven, there is no time, and Heaven's children are unaware of tomorrow or yesterday.

"Sorry again," said Peter.

She smiled. "Where are you off to?"

"Hawaii," said Peter, "my friends and I are going to study there. How about you? Do you live in San Diego?"

"I'm off to Bright Lights Illinois, to do a fashion show."

"Careful of the modeling runway, you wouldn't want to hurt yourself."

She frowned again but shook his hand and he walked on.

He got to the pier and headed for the cruise ship, to go up the gangplank and join his friends. As he walked and passed some of the shops that were on the pier, he saw some children running to a stand where it looked like there was a puppet show going on. Peter slowly walked up, and noticed a very old, yes, very old Ray the Taller and Ray the Shorter, doing a spectacular production of "Peter and the Schlurrg." That was the title posted on the makeshift marquee above their little booth. Ray the Taller looked out and saw Peter. It took a minute, but there was recognition. Ray the Shorter couldn't stand up anymore, but was still very good at telling the stories to the children from his chair, and he saw Peter as well.

"I was right," he said.

END NOTES

1. Reference to The Lion the Witch and the Wardrobe by C. S. Lewis copyright 1950 in Great Britain by Butler & Tanner Limited Frame for Geoffrey Bless Limited.

2. Douglas Adams as quoted by Andrew Wilson in his blog Thinktheology.co.uk Fairies and Gardens Wednesday the 4th 2012. In addition, the following reflection by this author is also the same as Wilson's and is unintentional, but credit is given to him here as well.

Lasting Greenlands
Obloomn
Peter's Journey
Starts Here
Folsborn
N
W
E
S
Sea of Folsborn
Covenswold
INNERWORLD

ABOUT THE AUTHOR

J. C. Egan (James Egan) is also an actor and completed his degree in Theatre Arts from California State University in the late 80's. At that same time, he became one of the founding members of the Santa Susana Repertory Company, now known as the Thousand Oaks Repertory Corporation. As a playwright he has written original plays and stage adaptations for the Repertory Company as well as plays and librettos for several churches. He published his first book, "Justus' Lament and Other Short Plays for Church Groups" in the early 2000s.

In addition to working on a few screenplays, he is currently finishing up a rock musical. His first novel, Tales of the Astro Force, is being revised for the Bright Lights series. Innerworld is part of the Bright Light series of satires that are warm and broad and that cover his favorite genres. His latest film effort was writing the lyrics to the animated musical, "The Promise: Birth of the Messiah" and is credited as lyrics consultant. He lives in the San Fernando Valley with his family.

You can follow him on Facebook, Twitter, Instagram, Good reads, IMDb and soon his own website, www.jceganauthor.com